"We must be sensible, Paul," Marny sighed

She drew herself out of his arms and walked to the fireplace. "Don't you remember what you said, Paul, about the life-giving element in passion being important? It *is* important. Far more than giving in to our feelings and cheapening our love."

"You're damnably right, of course," he growled, "but I am not particularly consoled." She turned to look at him and saw the grim smile curling the edges of his mouth.

"Our love," he repeated. "It's like saying our child, or our house, but we're never going to have a child together or live in a house together—we both know it."

He said bitterly, "You know as well as I that I can't let Ilena down; I daren't."

VIOLET WINSPEAR
is also the author of these books in

Harlequin Presents Collection

Many of these titles are available at your local bookseller.

VIOLET WINSPEAR

house of strangers

Originally published as Harlequin Presents #27

𝓗𝓪𝓻𝓵𝓮𝓺𝓾𝓲𝓷 𝓑𝓸𝓸𝓴𝓼

TORONTO • LONDON • LOS ANGELES • AMSTERDAM
SYDNEY • HAMBURG • PARIS • STOCKHOLM • ATHENS • TOKYO

Harlequin Presents edition published November 1973

ISBN 0-373-15017-2

Second printing July 1974
Third printing August 1974
Fourth printing May 1976
Fifth printing September 1976
Sixth printing February 1977
Seventh printing December 1978

This *Harlequin Presents Collection* edition published May 1981

Original hardcover edition published in 1963
by Mills & Boon Limited

CHAPTER I

THE evening before Marny Lester set out for London, where she was to work at the Stillman Clinic, the aunt and uncle with whom she had lived for a number of years gave a farewell dinner party for her. It wasn't a big party, for Marny disliked fuss and frills. Only the family and a few friends sat round the dining-table, and each one of them thought how young the girl looked to be setting out alone for life in the big city.

But Marny had been insistent about going, as she could be when she liked.

She loved Norfolk, of course, but she wanted the adventure of life in London, and that was why she had enrolled for the secretarial course at a Norwich business college when she had left school. It was all very well for Uncle Richard to say she had no need to work, but would she have enjoyed keeping busy just running around with Aunt Marjorie, who had all her fingers in the local pies and was for ever organizing fêtes and bazaars to help charitable causes? When Marny asked her uncle this, he had given that exasperating cough of his and replied that he, after all, was a man.

"I don't see what that's got to do with it." Marny had felt like pushing him over. "It would drive me cuckoo organizing fêtes and selling old clothes at jumble sales. I want the satisfaction of a good job as much as any man."

"Being a secretary isn't as easy as you seem to think, my girl." Out had come Uncle Richard's pompous, family-solicitor manner and behind his striped coat tails had gone his hands. "I'll guarantee that within two months you're running home to us, complaining that you're bored stiff with your 'great adventure.' I know you, Marny! You're as restless as your father was. He could never stick to one occupation for longer than a month or two."

"Anyway, I'm going to have a try, Uncle." Marny had thrust up her independent young chin. "Miss Grinham at the college has personally recommended me to the head of this clinic in London, and I think I shall find it much more exciting working for an osteopath than a business executive – or a family solicitor." Her green eyes had twinkled mischievously, but Richard Lester possessed little sense of humour and he had never fully understood his brother's only child. He thought her impertinent and rather odd in her ideas, and if the real truth be told he was relieved in a way that she was going away to London. His son Derek had always been fond of his cousin, and now the girl was nineteen, and beginning to look grown up, it was probably just as well that this job was going to separate them.

Marriage beween first cousins was never a good thing, and even the fact that Marny's concert pianist mother had left her a nice little bit of money couldn't alter the fact that she seemed the sort of girl who would never settle down to placid domesticity. She seemed to be stretching out her hands for something beyond Richard Lester's rather narrow concept of life, and he frowned when he thought of her bursts of gaiety, which shook the house when she sat down at the drawing-room piano and banged out those music-hall ballads his brother had taught her when she was quite a small child. Then at other times she would be strangely silent and go wandering off to the Broads, where she took out a boat and stayed away for hours, worrying the life out of her aunt and coming home with pussy-willows in her hair and her toreador pants wet to the thighs where she had been scrambling about in the water like a six-year-old.

6

She took after her father. There had been wanderer's dust in Glenn's shoes, and even after he had married and a child had quickly resulted he had never fully settled down. Richard Lester believed firmly that it was an Englishman's duty to settle down and be a law-abiding family man. He wanted Derek to live by this maxim, especially now he had been taken into the firm, and Marny would be an unsteadying influence on a young fellow rather than the reverse.

Marny's uncle glanced across the dining-table, and pursed his lips in disapproval. He could recall the suffragette marches, and his niece had some of the disturbing determination of those females in her fine-boned young face. A lift to her chin and a way of holding her slim body that denoted her independence of spirit, yet which also revealed how unawakened she was to an awareness of any man as an individual. She lumped them all together – domestic tyrants, determined to make wives and mothers of all women and so snatch their freedom from them.

She saw Derek like this, and she wrinkled a mocking nose at him when he told her across his glass of sherry that she should always wear green because she looked such a darling in the colour.

"Paul Stillman is a Canadian, I believe?" the Vicar said, smiling benignly upon this 'slender soldier of a girl,' as he called her, and quite forgetting tonight that she had trespassed into the Vicarage orchard more than once and filched pocketfuls of his prize pippins.

"That's right, Vicar." She had a clear, rather boyish voice. "Miss Grinham at the college has told me a great deal about him. He cures people by manipulating their bones and joints, and he employs a fairly large staff at the Clinic. The secretary he has had for some time had to go back to Canada to look after her father owing to her mother's sudden death. Miss Grinham got to hear he was in need of a new secretary and she recommended me for the job. She thought I'd enjoy working with him."

"I've heard of the celebrated bone-setter myself," put in Miss Courtfield from the Hall. Miss Courtfield had become acquainted with the Lesters through Marjorie's charitable activities, and now and again she honoured them with her presence at dinner. Marjorie and her husband thought of it as an honour, but Marny disliked the woman because she favoured blood sports.

"I hope you've heard some nice things, Miss Courtfield." Marny's green eyes rested on the woman's horsy face in that cool, direct way of hers.

"As a matter of fact I've heard he's a bit of a slave-driver, and I know for a fact that he's most impolite. A friend of mine got a nasty shoulder wrench in a fall she had at one of last year's meets, and someone suggested she go to Stillman. He wanted to know how she got the wrench, and when she told him, he casually rose to his feet and showed her to the door. And do you know what he had the audacity to say to her – and I mean she *is* Lady Mell's niece?" Miss Courtfield's indignant eyes travelled round the table. "He said he'd sooner treat the poor beast of a fox she'd been chasing than make her fit to chase another one."

Aunt Marjorie was pulling a suitably shocked face when Marny burst out laughing.

"Bravo, Mr. Stillman!" Her eyes were bright green with delight. "Miss Grinham said he had a razor edge to his tongue, and I'm all for him using it on people who chase small animals until they're mad with panic. It isn't sport! It's sheer perverted lust!"

"Marny!" Uncle Richard coughed warningly and inclined his head towards the Vicar. Derek nearly choked on a mouthful

8

of sherry and had to be thumped on the back by his cousin. Quite blithely she went on: "Don't you agree with me, Vicar? I mean, you preach about the sins of the flesh –"

Aunt Marjorie rose hurriedly to her feet. "I think, ladies, we'll go to the drawing-room and drink our coffee while the men enjoy a chat and a smoke. Marny," deadly emphasis upon the name, "I think you said earlier on that you would play the piano for us. Perhaps you will, when the men are ready to join us."

Marny did play for a while, and because she was really fond of Aunt Marjorie, whom she considered good-natured in a slightly silly fashion, she kept strictly to light music by Novello and Kern, though whenever she glanced at Miss Courtfield's horsy face she felt awfully like breaking into "The Galloping Major."

But she was far too excited about going away tomorrow to be able to sit at the piano for long, and in a while she excused herself and wandered out to the garden.

The garden was fresh after a summer shower, and Marny ran her fingers along the wet clipped hedges and breathed the scent of sleeping roses. She didn't hear footsteps come across the grass behind her, and she gave a startled gasp when warm hands found her shoulders and turned her around. Derek stood before her, and the moonlight made his face look rather pale.

"Moonlight and roses," he murmured. "Don't let's waste them." But when he would have pulled her against him, she wrenched free of his hands and sped away down the avenue formed by the clipped hedges. Fleet as she was, however, Derek was fleeter tonight, and he soon had her cornered under a rustling lime tree, slim and struggling in his urgent young arms.

"You're a beast, Derek Lester, and you've had too much to drink!" Marny drew back a silver-slippered foot and kicked

9

him hard on the shin. "Leave me alone, a-and go and paw Daisy Courtfield – she's just dying for it!"

"I'm not drunk, you little tigress." The boy laughed, excited by the struggling girl and the battle scar she had just inflicted on his shin. "It takes more than two glasses of sherry to do that to me. You're what's wrong with me, Marny. You're not a kid any longer – and you're darned fetching in this flimsy silk thing." He laid his warm face against her cool neck. "Let me kiss you. A kiss never hurt anyone."

She felt his lips searching her neck and she stamped hard on his foot. "If you don't let me go, Derek, I'll scream this garden down," she threatened.

"Don't go away tomorrow – stay and marry me," he whispered.

"I'm getting ready to scream – and I wouldn't marry you if you were the last man on earth! Why, you're laughable, Derek." Instinct had come to her aid, and she began to laugh with all the cruelty a girl can muster when a man's arms terrify her with their demanding strength. She felt her cousin's arms relax their hold on her, then he stood morosely thrusting the tumbled sandy hair back from his eyes.

"Oh, stop laughing like that," he mumbled.

"Well, you're a preposterous idiot." Now Marny knew herself in command of the situation she relaxed against the trunk of the lime. "We're first cousins, and your father doesn't approve of me one little bit. And apart from that I haven't the slightest urge to tie myself down to married life just yet."

She possessed a breakable slenderness there before her tall young cousin, but he saw the glint of adult laughter behind her clustering, leaf-brown lashes, and his hands slowly clenched at his sides. "You cold-blooded little fish!" he stormed. "I bet Daisy Courtfield would be a better proposition than you."

"I'm sure she would," Marny giggled. "She loves your freckles."

"Do you know what I hope, Marny?" Derek spoke through gritted teeth. "I hope you meet a man in London who tears your armour into a thousand little pieces and makes you chew them."

"You heartless devil, Derry!" And because they were good friends when he wasn't being amorous, Marny caught at his arms and gave him a fond shake. "Pack up all this silly love talk," she ordered. "I'm a career girl. I could never settle down to being a respectable solicitor's wife, and you know it. I want to go out into the world and do things, and when I'm twenty-one and Uncle Richard hands over my money I'm going to start travelling. Then later on I might even take seriously to the piano and become a concert pianist like my mother."

"You do play awfully well, Marny." Now Derek tucked his old comrade's arm about her, and feeling his gentleness, the slackened muscles which no longer felt like cords, Marny accepted his arm, and they leaned their backs against the big lime tree and dwelt in their seperate thoughts for a while.

Marny had lived with Derek's parents for eight years, ever since her own parents, crossing to Ireland one winter day to visit her grandmother, had been drowned when their steamer had gone down in the Irish Channel. When the headmistress of Marny's boarding-school had informed her of her parents' deaths, she had said: "Always remember, my dear, when we have good memories of those we love, they never completely die for us."

Marny still had good memories of her tall laughing father and her petite Irish mother, who had played the piano so beautifully. They had seemed the happiest two people in the world, and it wouldn't have been right for them to be separated,

11

even in death.

Then, as though her thought was communicated to Derek, that her father or her mother would have been left terribly lonely if death had claimed one and not the other, he said to her: "Don't you ever feel lonely, Marny? Don't you ever feel that you want somebody to belong exclusively to you? Shutting out the dark night? Keping you warm? Sharing all your innermost longings?"

Marny considered her cousin's words, and she knew without a doubt that her parents had found together the kind of love he talked about. That very rare kind of love, which is a mysterious sense of communication between two people. A subtle awareness of what hurts, pleases or delights the feelings of the other person. Generous, joyful, and unafraid to share the sorrowful moments when they came.

A very rare kind of love!

Marny, for instance, had never seen Uncle Richard laugh secret messages into Aunt Marjorie's eyes, the way her father had laughed them into her mother's. Nor did you ever see a flower pinned to Aunt Marjorie's dress and know that her husband had pinned it there. They were just two people who shared the same house with reasonable friendliness, but Marny felt certain they didn't share the same innermost longings. The way her aunt had taken all sorts of charitable causes to her heart was a sure sign that she felt the need to be wanted and was not fully wanted by her husband.

"Don't I attract you at all in a marriageable way, Marny?" Derek asked.

"No, Derry."

"You're wretchedly honest."

"I'm honest for your sake. I want you to be happy with the right girl, the only girl, and you'll bless me for turning you down when you eventually find her. Only, Derry dear, don't marry Daisy Courtfield on the rebound, will you?" She was laughing at him again, but this time he couldn't feel hurt. Nor could he, quite honestly, feel that he really loved her enough to want to marry her. It had been the wine, and the feel of her small bones under the silk of her dress, combined with the fact that she was going away tomorrow.

He smiled and dropped an affectionate kiss on her dark hair, whose softness tickled his lips. "Sorry I pestered you, you funny little monkey," he murmured. "Funny but wise. Stay wise, up there in London."

"Because of that someone who will want to tear my armour into a thousand pieces – and make me chew them?" She laughed gaily, "Just let him try!"

Paul Stillman had said in a letter to Marny that as she was a comparative stranger to London he would send someone from his Clinic to meet her at the railway station, and though she felt certain she'd have soon found the Clinic, which was near Regent's Park, she wrote back accepting his offer. She rather welcomed the opportunity of meeting a member of Paul Stillman's staff before she met him, for Miss Grinham, being a friend of his, might have been painting him in rosier colours than he deserved. She had spoken of him as a man dedicated to his chosen work, but fair-minded enough to make allowances for the fact that this would be Marny's first job.

"If you're unsuitable as a secretary he'll soon tell you," Miss Grinham had said. "But if you are suitable, then I think you'll find him an extremely interesting man to work for."

Marny hoped so, as she alighted on to the platform at Liverpool Street Station and accepted her suitcases from the friendly old farmer who had travelled most of the way with her. "Ever you be wantin' a job on a farm, you get in touch with me," he told her. "Jake Warner of Attleborough, everybody thereabouts knows me. Me and my missus could do with a lively lass like you about our place."

"I'll certainly keep your offer in mind, Mr. Warner," Marny assured him, then she smiled a gay goodbye at him and walked into the crowd that was surging towards the ticket barrier.

"I shall be wearing a green and black jockey cap and I have dark hair," she had written to Paul Stillman, "so the person you send to meet me shouldn't have a lot of trouble picking me out!"

Her jockey cap was poised jauntily over one eye, but she wasn't being given much chance to exhibit herself in it, for a group of very much larger people were jostling her willy-nilly towards the nearest exit and she had to battle her way clear of them. In the process she got herself and her suitcases entangled with a couple of bowler-hatted office types who were ready to be a bit too friendly, and then with a woman pulling a dog on a lead, neither of whom had the friendly dispositions of the two office types. Finally a careless arm knocked her jockey cap clean off her head.

"I never did!" Her green eyes flashed bright with exasperation. She made a dive for her cap, but a slender masculine hand was there before her and scooping it off the ground.

"A green and black jockey cap and dark hair," drawled a slightly grating voice, and Marny found herself gazing into a pair of amused grey eyes – very light, almost silvery eyes, set in a face which immediately struck her as being at once hard and yet humorous; attractive and yet ugly. In the very centre of the man's chin was the deepest cleft Marny had ever seen in her life, while slashing dark eyebrows and dark hair threw into startling relief those luminous eyes.

14

"You're Marny Lester, without a doubt," he said, and he plonked her cap on her head and imperiously swung her suitcases out of her hands.

"Just one moment!" Marny hung on the handles of her cases. "Are you from the Stillman Clinic?"

"Very much so." His lips twitched amusedly. "I'm Paul Stillman."

"Oh!"

"Oh?" He mimicked her startled expression rather unkindly. "What were you expecting, someone creaking with distinction and frosty at the temples?"

Marny slowly shook her head and thought of that foxhunting story which Daisy Courtfield had told at the dining-table last night. Paul Stillman looked that story from the top of his dark head (completely without any frosting) to the tips of his well-polished shoes. She just hadn't been expecting her employer to meet her in person.

"You wrote to say you were sending a member of your staff to meet me, Mr. Stillman," she explained. "That's why I'm surprised."

"I had to come into the West End, so I thought I'd collect my new secretary in person." His eyes dwelt on her tipsy cap. "Put that absurd thing straight, otherwise they won't let us into the Dorchester. We're lunching there."

Marny hurried along beside his tall, striding figure, adjusting her cap as she went. Lunch at the Dorchester! She smiled excitedly and followed Paul Stillman into the street, where he threw open the door of a black Bentley and tossed her cases into the back of it. The sunshine glittered on the chrome fittings of the car and splashed the red buses as they roared by. The fume of the city stung Marny's nostrils, fresh from the country, and her heart beat very fast under the short jacket of her green suit.

Paul Stillman stood beside his car watching her, and the thought came to him that she looked not unlike a small girl bedazzled by a bright shop window display. He frowned slightly. Miss Grinham had assured him that Marny Lester was intelligent, an excellent shorthand-typist and decidedly not the flirtatious sort who would learn the routine of the Clinic and then decide that she wanted to leave and marry some boy she had met at a dance. He hoped Miss Grinham was right, but he had his doubts. The girl was unusually decorative, and there was one particular member of his staff who was very partial to decorative females, especially young ones, up from the country and with the dew of innocence still clinging to them.

Then Marny grew aware that her employer was waiting for her to step into the car, and she smiled a quick apology at him and slipped into her seat. He climbed in beside her, long-legged but not awkward, and he didn't speak until they were clear of the heavy traffic in the vicinity of the station. Then he addressed her by her first name in the easy manner of a man who hadn't bothered about conventions at any time in his life.

"So this will be your first job, Marny?" he said. "Miss Grinham tells me she especially recommended you for my Clinic because she didn't feel you'd take happily to the orthodox routine of a nine-to-five-thirty office. Well, my routine isn't orthodox, and that's why I suggested you live in at the Clinic as my former secretary did. If I'm particularly tied up with a case during the day, you'll be expected to take letters in the evening. But this isn't as bad as it sounds." He shot a smile at her, showing square, rather boyish teeth. "You'll have time off during the day to sunbathe in Regent's Park. Or you can visit with the monkeys in the Zoo. But I repeat that I shall probably require you most evenings, so I hope you haven't a young man in London whom you'll want to go gallivanting with."

16

"No, I haven't a young man." She shook her head impatiently and a lock of her bright hair danced against her cheek. "Miss Grinham told me your routine was necessarily unorthodox owing to your clinical duties, but I shan't mind that." She regarded his hands on the wheel of the car, strong, slender, with beautifully kept fingernails. "Do you specialize in certain ailments, Mr. Stillman?"

"The spine is my particular baby." Then he frowned slightly. "I've a case at the Clinic right now which is occupying a great deal of my time – the young daughter of an attaché at the French Embassy, Nadia Justine. She was in ballet, but about two years ago she had a fall from the stage during a performance of *The Silver Dove*, that lovely thing by Ricci, and her spine was badly knocked about. She's been in the hands of lord knows how many specialists, and now her father has sent her to me. It was her father I had to come into the West End to see . . ." He broke off in that moment and drew the car to a standstill before the impressive façade of the Dorchester Hotel. A smart-looking commissionaire stepped forward and opened the car door, then Marny and Paul Stillman walked into the cocktail lounge of the hotel, where he immediately glanced round as though he were looking for someone.

Marny stared as a tall girl slid gracefully off a bar stool and came towards them. She trailed a mink stole at her heels like a pet dog on a lead, and her cream bouclé wool dress showed off the most exquisite figure Marny had ever seen. She had small, exotic features, a matt skin like white petals, and eyes that held all the petrol-blue colours in rain-wet slate, their slight almond shape adding a sort of Eastern mystery to her face. Beautifully dressed dark hair clung to her shapely head, while the heels of her tiny shoes were so high she seemed to tiptoe across the floor.

17

"Paul! Daarling!" The girl threw an arm about Paul Stillman's neck and kissed his mouth with a total disregard for either Marny's eyes or any other eyes. "You brute, you have kept me waiting ten minutes," she caressingly informed him. "I would not wait one minute for any other man, do you know that?"

"I should do, Ilena, you've told me so often enough." He grinned at her, then pulled Marny forward. "This is the young person you must blame for your ten-minute wait, honey. Her train was late getting in. Marny, meet Ilena Justine. I was telling you about her cousin coming along in the car."

Marny held out a hand to the exquisite French girl, but Ilena coolly ignored it. "Your new secretary, Paul?" Her almond-shaped eyes moved over Marny's face and they smiled slightly at the shiny tip to the other girl's nose. Then she caught possessively at Paul's arm. "Daarling, I am sinking at the midriff, so do let us go in and have luncheon." She pouted her scarlet mouth at him. "I want truffles, some nice breast of chicken and braised celery."

"Ilena, I believe food's the only thing you ever think about with any real interest," he drawled.

"That is not true, Paul." She touched the cleft in his chin, and Marny saw the white gleam of her tiny teeth between her very red lips. "I've my hat shop in Bruton Street to worry about. I have Nadia and Uncle Henri. And you, of course, chéri."

"What a shockingly complicated life," he mocked. "No wonder you need building up with truffles and chicken." He led her out of the cocktail lounge, and Marny followed them, feeling a bit of a gooseberry.

But over a really delicious lunch Paul saw to it that Marny wasn't excluded from the conversation, though it was obvious

18

that Ilena Justine thought her of very little account. They were drinking their coffee when she said to Marny: "Your hair must be a terrible trial to you, it looks so full of electricity. And do you know, *petite*, those jockey caps are now quite out of mode . . ."

"Ilena," the grating quality of Paul Stillman's voice was suddenly very noticeable, "one of these days I'm going to turn you over my knee and give you the sound spanking your indulgent guardian of an uncle has never bothered to apply!"

"Really, darling?" Ilena blinked long interested lashes at him. "Would you not be afraid that I would stop loving you if you did such a brutal thing to me?"

"You're just dying to be scragged, you little throwback to the cave-days," he laughed. "That's why I appeal to you. I don't pamper you the way all the other men in your life have pampered you." As he spoke, Marny saw him touch the big square-cut diamond ring on Ilena's engagement finger. Marny had noticed the ring of course, but somehow she hadn't connected its meaning with Paul Stillman, despite the rather abandoned way Ilena had embraced him in the cocktail lounge. Now, as his slender fingers played with the dazzling stone, it came home to her that it was he who had put the ring on the French girl's elegant little hand with its poppy-red fingernails. She realized that her employer was engaged to Ilena.

"Why did you go to see Uncle Henri this morning?" Ilena asked him.

"Someone's been telling him I use witchcraft . . . yeah, you might well laugh, honey, though it's a joke that's beginning to wear a bit thin with me. I'm an osteopath and damned proud of the fact."

"Of course you are, *chéri*," Ilena cooed. "Now tell me calmly what happened."

19

"Well, some pill-pedlar in Harley Stret has been telling your uncle that he's put Nadia in the gravest danger, putting her in my hands. Henri was at the Clinic last night – the one night I give myself a few hours off – and he's gone and communicated his loss of confidence in me to Nadia. I must have her confidence if I'm to help her, and I've told Henri he either lets me have complete charge of her, with no interference, or he takes her away."

"Poor Uncle! You no doubt frightened the life out of him?"

"No doubt!" Paul proffered Ilena a cigarette, while Marny's little shake of the head made him smile, half to himself. "You're nineteen, aren't you, Marny?" he said.

"Yes." She had seen him smile, and she belatedly wished she'd accepted a cigarette and that she hadn't worn this darn jockey cap. She must look a complete kid beside Ilena Justine!

"Nadia's about the same age," Paul's grey eyes were looking rather keen. "D'you know, it might be a big help to the kid to have someone of her own age to talk to at the Clinic. I'll see to it that you meet her, Marny. You might find you have interests in common."

"If Nadia was a dancer, then she probably likes music. I like music myself." Marny spoke eagerly, excited by the thought that she was being invited to help Paul Stillman with one of his most difficult patients. A patient who had caught her sympathy in his car, when he had said the girl had been hurt while dancing in *The Silver Dove*. It was curious and intriguing, for that ballet was the story of a dove who broke its wing and couldn't fly with the other birds in search of a mate.

After lunch Paul dropped his fiancée off at her smart little hat shop in Bruton Stret, then he and Marny drove to the Clinic.

It was situated in a quiet square facing Regent's Park, white-

20

stoned and with tall Corinthian pillars at the front entrance. They walked into the large cool hall, and Marny blinked when a furry bundle of a cat hurled itself at Paul rather in the manner of a dog and the next moment had climbed to his shoulder.

"You're wearing a smug look, Tiger," Paul said to the handsome animal. "Where have you been, out courting as usual?"

Marny checked a little grin and was looking, she hoped, suitably secretarial when Paul said to her: "We'll go to my office and I'll get one of my nurses to come and take you across to the bungalow where you'll be living."

"The bungalow?" Marny looked intrigued.

He nodded. "It's built in the Canadian style. All modern installations, and rather nicer for the nurses than always being here among their patients."

The room he termed his office was more like a well-lived-in den, with big leather armchairs worn to comfortable proportions, plenty of books, a strong scent of cigars, and a rather littered desk. Paul swept aside some of the litter and took up the receiver of the house phone. He asked for a Nurse Truscott and watched Marny's interested examination of his office.

"Is this where we'll be working, Mr. Stillman?" she asked.

"Yes." He broke into a grin. "I hope you weren't expecting tubular furniture and rubber plants?"

"No, indeed! I like your office just as it is," Marny quickly assured him.

"Which is just as well, for I'm a bit of an untidy devil . . . ah, is that you, Scotty?" He spoke into the receiver of the phone. "I've got Miss Lester with me and I'd like you to help her settle in, if you will? Swell. Say, how's number ten? Has that new injection helped his knee – it hasn't? H'm, that isn't good. I think I'll get Dennis to take some more pictures. If you see him on your way down, bring him along with you, Scotty."

21

Marny had wandered over to the glass doors that looked out on to the surprisingly extensive grounds of the Clinic, and her employer came and stood behind her after he had stopped speaking on the phone. "D'you see that clump of trees, Marny?" He directed her attention towards them with a slender hand. "The nurses' bungalow is just beyond them. You can just see the corner of it."

"Why, it's rather like a big Swiss chalet," she exclaimed, turning to smile up at him. He was very tall when you stood near him, she realized, and his light grey eyes had a disturbing clarity under his dark eyebrows. They were penetrating, rather quizzical eyes, and right now there was a twinkle in them.

"I hope you aren't going to disrupt my staff – the male half," he drawled. "Miss Grinham failed to tell me that my new secretary was an attractive redhead with green eyes."

"Miss Grinham didn't think you'd mind about my age just as long as my shorthand and typing were up to standard – and they are!" Marny's young chin was firmly thrust up. "And I can assure you I have no intention of disrupting the male members of your staff. I couldn't care less about men!"

"Really." His lips twitched. "An agreeable sentiment in a secretary, if true. What do you care about, then, apart from music? I recall that you said you liked music while we were talking at the Dorchester."

"I like walking and sailing, things like that," she told him.

"The open-air type, huh?"

"I suppose so."

"Then whatever made you think you'd like working in London, behind a desk?"

"A girl can't just rusticate," she objected, "and when Miss Grinham told me about this job and got it for me, I just couldn't wait to get here and start it." Marny's eyes were fixed upon her employer's face; young, eager eyes, lustrous as green jewels. "I – I want to tell you how pleased I felt, Mr. Stillman, when you said I might meet Nadia Justine and try to help with her. I want to be of help. I want to be useful. And I feel in my bones that I can be."

"Well, I'm all for enthusiasm, and I can see you're a vital, willing young specimen." Paul smiled, and for a brief moment one of his mobile hands was upon her hair, brushing its springing waves back from her eyes. "H'm, I think you'll be good for Nadia. Yes, I certainly think you can help there. She's hopelessly depressed, poor girl . . ."

He broke off at that juncture, for there was a tap on the door and it opened to admit a plump, middle-aged nurse, followed by a young man in a white overall.

"Scotty, come and meet my new secretary," Paul invited, and though Nurse Truscott's eyes flashed with unmistakable surprise when they first rested on Marny, they were full of friendliness when she held out a hand to her. "How do you do, Miss Lester." The nurse spoke in a strange Canadian accent. "I sure hope you're going to be happy here at the Clinic with us."

"You can say that again, Scotty," put in the young man in the white overall. He was looking straight at Marny as he spoke, and she saw that his face was dark and lean and strikingly handsome. His black eyebrows, above tawny eyes, were amusingly mobile; the kind of eyebrows that moved in conjunction with all he thought and said, while his mouth was quirked on a smile that echoed the gleam of wicked fun in his eyes.

"Marny, this is Errol Dennis. He's in charge of our X-ray department." Paul Stillman's voice wasn't too cordial as he made the introduction, while he took cold notice of the way the handsome Irishman held Marny's hand in both of his.

23

"Of course, with eyes as bright and green as the slopes of County Mayo, then you must be a countrywoman of mine," Errol said to her, and he smiled straight into her green eyes. "Now it's the truth I'm speaking, isn't it?"

"Partly," she agreed, and the crinkled edges of his tawny eyes made smiling back at him irresistible. "My mother was Irish."

"Sure, there's no mistaking the touch of the old Emerald Isle, God bless it!" His wiry fingers tightened on hers and she felt the pressure of the rather heavy ring he wore. "Welcome to our celebrated bone-factory, my dear."

Marny immediately felt the hostile tensing of Paul Stillman's tall figure beside her. At once she pulled her fingers free of the Irishman's and saw his mobile eyebrows mock the action. . . .

Then, with a rather shocking suddenness, the door of the office was jerked open and a young nurse came stumbling into the room. She was white-faced and thoroughly frightened, but it wasn't her face alone that held the eyes, fixed them, then fill them with quick horror. It was the bright splashes of blood marking the front of her pale blue uniform.

"Mr. Stillman – oh, sir –" she cried out, "you must come up to Nadia Justine's room right away! She – she's slashed her wrists with a pair of scissors!"

CHAPTER II

A SHOCKED silence greeted the young nurse's distracted words, then Paul Stillman was plunging past Marny out of the door. Nurse Truscott hurried after him, while the nurse in the blood-stained uniform seemed suddenly powerless to move. Her panicky eyes were fixed upon Errol Dennis's face, and it was as though she waited to be reassured, even comforted. He didn't move, and when Marny took a sympathetic step towards the girl, she turned and darted away, the rubber soles of her shoes silencing her flight across the hall to the stairs.

A French newspaper was sprawled on the floor beside Nadia's bed, but Paul was too busy applying tourniquets to her slashed wrists to notice it. When the young nurse saw it, she quickly thrust it into Nadia's bedside cabinet.

"You darn little fool!" Paul grated at Nadia, who moaned with pain and weakly fought him. "You're very much mistaken if you think you're getting away with a silly trick like this. You're going to live, my girl. And walk! D'you hear me?"

His face above the girl's was harsh, and his eyes blazed with anger. "Paul, let me go . . . let me die!" Nadia tore her gaping left wrist free of his fingers and tried to crash it against the side of the bed.

"Brelson – hold her!" The young nurse quickly obeyed, holding the thin, trembling shoulders of the French girl while Paul secured the tourniquet on her wrist and Nurse Truscott handed him a loaded hypodermic. "She'll need a transfusion," he said, withdrawing the needle from Nadia's arm as she relaxed into a white-faced stillness. "Phone the blood-bank for two pints, that should just about cover it, then I'll need you in the theatre, Scotty. These wrists must be stitched."

Nurse Truscott looked decidedly worried when she returned to Paul's office and plucked the receiver off the outside phone. "Errol, find me Miss Justine's filing card," she said, with her hand over the receiver. "I want to know her blood group. We always list it, thank the lord!"

"It's as bad as that, eh, Scotty?" He whipped open the box of filing cards and went through them with quick fingers. He gave Nurse Truscott the required group and he and Marny listened as the nurse requested the blood-bank to send the blood to the Clinic right away.

"It's her left wrist," she explained to Errol. "She's damaged it real bad, being right-handed, and she's lost a helluva lot of blood. The boss is raging."

Errol Dennis looked sardonic. "I bet he is! He'll have a fit and never come out of it if that kid dies of self-inflicted wounds on these hallowed premises. Think of all the lurid publicity. Very bad for our good name."

Nurse Truscott gazed back at Errol, and Marny saw a look of antagonism spring into her eyes. "*Our* good name, Errol?" she asked. "It's a mighty big surprise to me that you ever took the Clinic so much to heart. The almighty generous salary you get paid, no doubt, but none of the good work we do here. It amazes me that you stay on here. It's perfectly obvious you dislike taking orders from Mr. Stillman."

"Mr. Stillman?" He raised his eyebrows at her, a trifle jeeringly. "Now we all know it's Paul, in private, don't we, Scotty? We all know the pair of you are very, very good friends."

She flushed slightly at this remark, then she turned a shoulder on him and spoke to Marny. "Look, Miss Lester, honey, I must get back upstairs – Mr. Stillman's got to stitch up that

26

foolish kid's wrists – so I'll round up somebody else to take you across to our living quarters. Say," she studied the perplexed expression on Marny's face, "is there anything wrong? You look real troubled about something."

"Well, I am a bit puzzled," Marny admitted. "You said just now that Mr. Stillman was going to stitch Nadia's wrists. I didn't think he – well, osteopaths don't usually have anything to do with surgery, do they."

"Mr. Stillman doesn't practise surgery, no, but he's qualified to do so. Didn't you know? You didn't! Well, he started out as a surgeon, back in Toronto, and that's where I first met him, for we were both working at the same hospital. Then his older brother developed some sort of spinal trouble and it led him towards an interest in osteopathy, especially so after his brother got cured. He came over here and studied under Sir Austin Orde – that great old guy who was one of the first osteopath crusaders – and he kind of got wrapped up in England. When Sir Austin died and left him a sizeable bit of money he started this Clinic. Paul – Mr. Stillman's almighty proud of this place. I wouldn't like for this Nadia Justine business to put a damper on it."

"Come, come, Scotty," it was Errol Dennis who spoke, "what's the use of an influential prospective pa-in-law if you're not prepared to use him – and I'm darn sure Stillman will use him to hush up Nadia's attempt at suicide."

"And who would blame him?" Nurse Truscott defended stoutly.

"Not you, my hearty, that's for sure," Errol laughed. "What *has* Stillman got that makes you women knuckle under to him like a bunch of harem slaves? Would it be a touch of the devil, Scotty. That little something women can't resist."

"It's you that's got the devil touch, Errol Dennis," she shot back, and her starched skirts crackled with disapproval as she marched from the room.

It was fairly certain, the following morning, that Errol had been right in his guess and that Paul Stillman had used Monsieur Justine's influence to hush up the unhappy business of Nadia's wrist-slashing. There was no mention of it in the morning papers, Marny went through them especially to see, and she told herself that if the story wasn't in the *Daily Wire*, the most wide-awake paper of the lot, then it had been successfully covered up. And she knew a little glow of relief, for already she was beginning to identify herself with the affairs of the Clinic.

She was reading the *Daily Wire* in the charming, very modern breakfast-room of the nurses' bungalow. Sunshine splashed bright through the big, square windows and fell on to her, and she looked lissom and fresh in a white linen dress with a bronze coloured belt and shoes to match.

"Did you sleep well, Miss Lester?" asked one of the nurses, and when Marny glanced up, she found herself looking at the girl who had come running to the office yesterday, her eyes panicky and distracted. Now, Marny saw, she was rather a pert creature. Cyclamen lipstick and touched-up blonde hair made her look a little cheap and artificial, like a nurse in a film, but she seemed to want to be friendly, so Marny smiled back at her warmly.

"Yes, I slept fairly well, thank you," she said. "But I couldn't help worrying about Miss Justine. Have you heard how she is this morning?"

"Oh, she's all right. Mr. Stillman stayed with her the best part of the night, so you should be all right for some free time this morning. I expect he'll want to sleep."

But no sooner had she finished speaking than the house-phone buzzed out in the pine-panelled hall of the bungalow, and a minute later a nurse put her head round the door of the breakfast-room and told Marny she was wanted over in the office as soon as she had eaten breakfast.

"And the boss doesn't sound in a very cushy mood, love, so watch your step," the nurse advised, as she withdrew her head.

Marny's companion at the breakfast-table pulled a face, hitched up the skirt of her attractive uniform and examined a catch in one of her dark nylon stockings. "I expect he's been talking on the phone to the Imperial Princess," she said. Then she laughed at Marny's puzzled face. "I thought you'd met her. Didn't you have lunch with her and the boss at the Dorchester yesterday?"

"Oh, you're talking about Ilena, his fiancée!" Marny's impish smile spread over her face. "Well, I must admit the term suits her. She does act rather like a – a princess out of some imperial court. And she has a wonderfully casual manner with a mink stole."

"Actually – and by the way my name's Julie Brelson – actually there is a dash of royal blood in the Justines. Their grandmother was distantly related to the last Russian Czar, and when the revolution came, she and other members of her family fled to Paris, where she eventually married a Frenchman. Ilena Justine looks Russian, I think. And Nadia used to dance in ballet."

"I feel sorry for Nadia, even though I've never met her," Marny said. "Is she like Ilena?"

Julie shook her head. "No, she isn't a patch on Ilena for looks."

"I mean in her ways."

"Well," Julie considered, "she can be a bit high and mighty when she likes, but she isn't catty. Ilena's a shocking little cat, the sort who doesn't only notice if you've got a run in your

29

nylons, but who mentions it. But she doesn't come it with the boss." Julie broke into a spurt of laughter. "She's met her match in him all right."

"Have they been engaged very long?"

"A month or two, though he's known her a goodish while. It was a bit romantic the way they met. His brother and sister-in-law, and their young daughter, were over here on holiday, and all four of them went to a gala do at Covent Garden – Victoria de los Angeles was singing, I believe, and he's a bit partial to that kind of voice. Well, during one of the intervals Mr. Stillman and his brother went out to the foyer to smoke and Ilena Justine was there, doubled up on the floor! She wears ever such high-heeled shoes, as you may have noticed, and she'd fallen over and pulled a tendon in the back of one of her legs. She was in a lot of pain, but the boss soon put that right, as you can imagine, and he dated her up then and there and they've been going steady ever since. She's the one who persuaded him to have Nadia here, though I don't know whether he'll ever be able to do anything for her. A lot of other people have tried, really big specialists, you know, but her legs are just like logs. You can't help feeling sorry for her."

"I think she's had a raw deal!" Marny exclaimed.

"You'll get a raw deal yourself if you don't get over to the office," Julie laughed. "The boss has got a vile temper, you know, when he's put out – and you should see his eyes! Talk about grey ice!"

But when Marny reached Paul Stillman's office, the door was standing ajar and she hesitated outside, hearing voices, the raised voices of her employer and a man who spoke with a French accent.

"I had no idea, no idea at all that Nadia was still corresponding with this man. I had forbidden the continuance of the association. I had political reasons for doing so, for there was always a suspicion that he was an active Communist," stormed the Frenchman. "She wanted, at one time, for me to agree to their engagement. Faugh! The very idea! She – as she is! And that – that treacherous young fool!"

"Henri, would it really have rubbed much skin off your nose to have let that poor kid have her romance?" Paul Stillman broke in.

"*Mon ami*," Henri Justine sounded outraged, "I had the same reason for hushing up such an association as you have for hushing up Nadia's attempted suicide, because it would not do my career any good."

"One below the belt, Henri, but the point's taken." Paul's grating voice held a tinge of wry humour.

"What I can't understand is how she got hold of a French newspaper. I appealed to you to keep them from her, for Ilena and I both knew that René Blanchard had been sent for trial and that it would be recorded. We knew that if Nadia read of this, she would be upset. One of your nurses must have brought the paper in for her."

"Undoubtedly," Paul agreed. "But I can't trail around behind them all the time, and I don't suppose the foolish woman had any idea that Nadia would plunge a pair of nail scissors into her wrists when she read about Blanchard. I don't suppose she could even read the paper herself. I don't hire my nurses for their linguistic ability."

"It might be advisable to hire a more obedient type," Henri Justine suggested, with a touch of Ilena's waspishness.

"My nurses suit me," sudden arrogance rang in Paul's voice. "They're a pretty nice bunch of women, hard-working and conscientious, and if, now and again, one of them thumbs her nose at a piece of dictum I lay down, well, that's the way of women all the world over, isn't it. That's part of their damned cuteness, and I wouldn't have it any other way." Then he laughed a little. "Henri, would you call Ilena the obedient type?" he asked.

"We are not discussing Ilena," Henri Justine retorted. "We are discussing Nadia. My poor, foolish Nadia!"

"Yeah!" Paul drew a sudden harsh sigh. "This Blanchard business is going to make it harder than ever for us to pump some spirit into her . . ."

Marny, absorbed in that conversation, hadn't noticed that her employer's cat, the big tabby, had strolled out of his office. Now, seeing her and deciding to extend a bit of friendship, he came and rubbed himself against her legs. The action so startled her that she let out a little gasp, and Paul, in the office, heard it. He strode past Henri Justine and jerked the door wide open. He stared at Marny, impatiently thrusting the dark hair back off his forehead.

"Y-you phoned over for me," she said, and an embarrassed flush stole out of the neck of her white dress and flooded her face. She hadn't meant to eavesdrop, but she had become so interested in Nadia Justine's affairs that the mention of her name had riveted her attention and made it impossible for her to withdraw it.

"So I did." He spoke curtly, and his eyes were tired, with little lines etched at the sides of them. He seemed, in fact, to have a bad headache, for as he regarded Marny, he almost winced against the sunlight as it shafted through the hall windows. "I want you to take some letters and to help me with some other work. The letters should have gone off last night, but naturally I was tied up with Nadia. Come in!" He gestured rather impatiently and she walked past him into the office. Henri Justine, portly, but very well groomed, was smoking a cigarette by the long glass doors that looked on to the grounds. Paul introduced him to Marny. He acknowledged the introduction a trifle absently.

"Nadia will be all right, won't she, Paul?" he said.

"Oh, she isn't going to die, if that's what you mean," Paul replied. "It's her state of mind I'm worried about."

"May I go up and see her?"

"No."

"I beg your pardon!" Nadia's father dragged his cigarette-holder from his mouth. "What do you mean by saying no?"

"What does no usually mean? You saw her last night."

"But I want to see her now. I insist upon seeing her."

"Henri," Paul spoke with an abrupt weariness, "the kid's asleep and I don't want her disturbed. Leave her be. Leave her in peace for a while. Go back to the Embassy, or go to Ilena's place and let me get on with some work. I've about a dozen letters to dictate, three cases to attend to, and an appointment at one o'clock with the Matron of St. Patrick's Orphanage. They've a child there I'm interested in treating."

"But, *mon ami*, Nadia is *my* child," Henri Justine appealed. "Let me just assure myself that she is really going to be all right."

Paul's eyes half closed in weary exasperation, and then he smiled slightly. "Now I know where Ilena gets her obstinacy from! All right, come and see Nadia, but if you damn well wake her up, Henri, I'll toss you out of the Clinic on your ear, and that will really cause a rumpus at the Embassy." He turned to Marny. "I shan't be long, honey. Perhaps you'll give the kitchen a buzz and ask them to send in some coffee. Hot and strong, mind."

Then he and Nadia's father went upstairs, and after Marny had ordered the coffee, she sat down in one of her employer's

33

armchairs and tried to collect her thoughts into some sort of order, for they were jumping around like gnats in a tree. So Nadia had attempted to kill herself because a young man she was fond of had been accused of planting a bomb in a University building. And one of the nurses at the Clinic had supplied the newspaper which had carried the story of his trial.

Marny let her head rest in the comfortable dip Paul Stillman's head had worn into the leather of the chair and, for some reason, she found herself thinking of the way Julie Brelson had acted yesterday. Surely, for a nurse, she had displayed a great deal of panic? And she had looked at Errol Dennis as though she would have confided something to him, or asked him to comfort her, if there had been nobody else present. There was also something about her that suggested she might be susceptible to bribery, and it was obvious that the Justines were moneyed people. If Nadia had money with her, perhaps she had paid Julie to buy French newspapers for her? Oh, it was all very intriguing, and though Marny had been at the Clinic less than twenty-four hours, she already felt interwoven into its affairs and thoroughly interested in its occupants.

A few minutes later Paul Stillman came back to the office. His coffee had been brought in and he lay back in his chair behind the big desk and let Marny wait on him. He declined to take milk in his coffee, but when she handed him the cup, he liberally supplied it with sugar and drank its scalding blackness with obvious enjoyment.

"Ah, I needed that, Marny! Now let's get cracking with some work."

Marny was really surprised at the amount of paper work that running a place like this seemed to involve. There was the staff income-tax to be worked out, as it was Thursday and they'd be paid the following day. Bills to be checked and accounts met. Letters to answer. The office ledgers to keep in order. New equipment to be sent for. And Marny and Paul Stillman worked steadily until the clock on the mantelpiece chimed twelve times, and he glanced up sharply.

"Hell and high water, is that the time?" he exclaimed. They had been in the middle of a letter, but now he told Marny it would have to wait until later. He got to his feet. "I've a couple of patients I must see this morning, and I expect you heard me tell Monsieur Justine that I've an appointment to see the Matron of St. Patrick's Orphanage?"

Marny nodded and closed her shorthand pad. "About a little boy, didn't you say, Mr. Stillman?"

"Yeah." He took a well-handled cigar-case out of his pocket and selected a dark cigar from it. He bit off the end with his square, white teeth and applied a match to it. As he puffed the aromatic smoke, he seemed to relax for the first time that morning. "Yeah, a poor little scrap of a kid. The father, a drunken brute of a docker who was recently killed in a dock accident, was always knocking his wife about, but she finally ran out on him and he turned his attention to the boy. Now, as the result of a brutal beating, the boy carries one shoulder higher than the other. I want to try and help him. He's a plucky little guy, and there are indications that with the help of some surgery I might be able to put things right for him. I got to hear about him through Matron of the Home. She was a patient of mine a couple of years ago. She's had a talk with the members of the orphanage board and she's going to let me know today whether I can bring Ginger to the Clinic." Paul's eyes rested on Marny. "Do you get on well with children, Marny?" he asked.

"We-ell, I get on well with all sorts of animals." Her smile flashed. "There isn't a lot of difference, is there? Same high spirits, same need of understanding and protection."

35

He looked interested. "You're rather older than your years in lots of respects, aren't you?" he said. "Do you think you're going to enjoy working here?"

"Yes!" Just the one word, but the amount of warmth and assurance she put into it brought a quick, charming smile to Paul Stillman's face. Marny, taking note of that smile suddenly realized why this man appealed to the beautiful, seductive Ilena Justine, who seemed to have the world at her feet. He wasn't handsome, but there was about him an arresting, vital aliveness of body and mind, combined with an air of worldly experience. He had known quite a few women, Marny decided, but not thoughtlessly, as a rake knows them. He had taken the trouble to understand women's minds, as well as to appreciate their bodies, and he had emerged as a man with an exciting, knowledgeable personality. You could turn to him if you had troubles. You could tell him a joke. You could also be certain he'd be a frightening enemy if you ever did damage to anyone, or anything, he held dear.

Miss Grinham had told Marny he was thirty-six, yet when he smiled as he had just smiled, he looked curiously boyish. Or perhaps it was the unruly lock of dark hair that would keep falling into his left eye that made him look that way.

"I'm glad this upset we've had with Nadia Justine hasn't frightened you, Marny," he said. His eyes twinkled. "I take it you overheard all about René Blanchard, the hot-headed young fool she's in love with?"

Marny looked shamefaced. "I'm sorry, Mr. Stillman, for listening outside the door, but it wasn't just nosiness that made me listen. I feel genuinely sorry for Nadia. She seems fated to have her life messed up, first that fearful accident and now by this trouble her young man has got into."

"Damned young idiot!" In his exasperation Paul lost half

a finger of ash off his cigar and it spilled in a grey rain down the right leg of his trousers. "There may be a lot that wants putting right in the universities, but it isn't put right by organising the smuggling of arms to hot-headed groups of student agitators, which is what Blanchard has been doing. I guess when Nadia read this about him, she just couldn't face knowing she'd given her heart to a man who could consider blowing up innocent people." He glanced at his wrist watch. "And now I'd better be getting upstairs. When you've typed out that batch of letters, Marny, get them posted, then take yourself out for a stroll. I shall probably want you for an hour or two tonight."

"All right, Mr. Stillman."

He had begun to turn away, but suddenly he glanced back at her with a glint of enquiry in his eyes. "Has Errol Dennis tried to date you yet?" he asked.

She looked startled. "N-no, Mr. Stillman!"

"He probably will try, and if you're a wise young person, you'll steer clear of him."

"I intend to do just that." She looked straight back into the grey, enquiring eyes, and the tilt to her chin was both determined and indignant. "I told you yesterday that I had very little interest in men."

"An attitude of mind which our handsome Errol will thoroughly enjoy changing." Paul's eyes travelled over Marny, taking in the soft dark hair, the green eyes, slightly tilted nose and youth-flushed mouth. He saw the slightness of her waist, embraced by the bronze belt, the delicate lift of her breasts under the white linen of her dress, and the slenderness of her legs. She was quite delectable, he thought, and so youthfully vulnerable. He strolled to the door and opened it. "I'll see you later, Marny. Go and catch some sun, won't you?"

It was a bright, golden afternoon, with a fragrance of June clover in the air, and Marny was very ready to take advantage of her employer's suggestion that she go for a stroll and catch some sunshine.

She wandered into Regent's Park, and after exploring its leafy lanes for a while, she found a patch of sunlit grass and sat down upon it. She watched the people who had brought their dogs for a gambol in the park, and smiled at a couple of schoolboys who were flying an enormous kite. Suddenly the scarlet kite flirted its streamers in the sky and broke loose from the boys, and in an instant Marny was upon her feet and helping to chase the kite. She caught hold of its string with a gay shout of victory, and they were only too pleased to allow her to join in their fun. They had noticed she was alone and that she seemed a jolly sort.

Unselfconsciously she ran about the grass with the two boys, whooping at the kite's antics, and quite unaware that she was being observed with a great deal of interest and amusement by Errol Dennis, who was off duty this afternoon. He was stretched on his side in the warm grass, some yards away, a cigarette at a negligent angle in his mouth and his white shirt thrown open at his tanned throat. He looked darkly handsome, and several girls glanced at him with smiling interest as they passed by, but the whole of his attention was concerned upon Marny. She was laughing with the gay abandon of a child, the white skirt of her dress lifting above her knees as she and the boys lost the kite again and they went diving across the grass after it.

Errol's eyes suddenly glowed. He tossed his cigarette from him, leapt lithely to his feet and joined in the race for the kite. There was something of the faun about him, a hint of the pagan in his laughing, Irish face, and Marny saw this as his white shirt flashed past her and he captured the string of the kite just as it

38

was about to soar into a clump of tall oak trees.

"Cor, mister, thanks!" gasped one of the boys, watching with relieved, admiring eyes as Errol expertly drew the kite free of the trees and next moment had it gaily fluttering across the sky.

"Where did you spring from?" Marny demanded.

"Out of the nether regions!" His eyes laughed into hers, and only a girl fashioned from stone could have resisted the way he looked, with the sun on his throat and his arms, and the glow of an animal vitality in his tawny eyes. "May I play?" he wheedled. "Kites are a weakness of mine."

"You'd better ask the boys," she laughed, "it's their kite."

"Oh, your feller can play with us, miss," piped up a boyish voice, and Errol chuckled as he thanked the urchin, who had somehow managed to acquire the dirtiest face Errol had seen for a long time.

Marny and Errol played with the boys and their kite until they had to go home to their tea, and by that time Marny's hair was looking wildly abandoned and her green eyes sparkled into Errol's as she turned from waving good-bye to the boys. "That was fun!" she exclaimed, and she threw herself down on the grass and he joined her.

"Cigarette?" He extended his case and she accepted one.

"I'm afraid I shall never grow up," she laughed, as she dipped her head to his lighter.

"No, don't ever grow up." Cigarette smoke drifted past his eyes as they rested on her, with appreciation. "Stay a child of nature for always. It suits you."

"I'm sure I look a sight," she retorted, but she made no attempt to smooth her hair. She lay back lazily in the grass, contentedly smoking her cigarette and feeling the warm touch of the sun on her bare legs and arms. Through her lashes she watched a few fleecy clouds drift across the blue sky, and there was no consciousness in her of Errol Dennis as anything more than a companionable boy, like her cousin Derek. She had quite forgotten in this moment that Derek had managed to frighten her with his sudden revealing, the other evening, of instincts that were not boyish.

"Yes, a sight for sore eyes," Errol told her, and he touched a light finger to her tip-tilted nose. "You baby, how did you manage to persuade your people to let you leave the fold to come into this untamed forest called London? Wasn't Mother scared for her pet lamb?"

"My mother died eight years ago, along with my father."

"I say, that was bad luck!" He looked sympathetic, and she explained about the steamer that had gone down in the Irish Channel, taking those two delightful people out of her life. "Still, I've never forgotten them," she said. "While I had them, I had real happiness. I was very lucky. Lots of children seem to be born into homes where they're not really wanted, but I was wanted, utterly and completely, and it was a wonderful feeling."

"Marny the love-child," Errol murmured, in his caressing Irish voice, and Marny didn't notice right away that he had covered her hand with his as it lay in the grass. "Marny's a rare sort of name. How did you come by it?"

"It's a combination of my parents' names," she explained. "My father's name was Glenn, but Mother always called him Glenny. Her name was Mary, so they put the two together and Marny was the result." And now Marny became aware of the pressure of Errol's hand and she slipped free of it. "Don't — don't flirt with me. Just be friends," she begged.

"Can't people flirt and yet remain friends?" he asked, softly and mockingly.

"No." She shook her head and her hair had a vibrant lustre

in the sunshine. "Men start off by just flirting, then they — they —"

"Can't you say it?" He grinned through his cigarette smoke. "They want to kiss and cuddle. Well, there isn't any harm in any of that. It's all rather delicious . . . for the girl as well as the man."

"Oh, you!" She leapt to her feet and began to hurry away from him, tossing her cigarette out of her hand. He caught up with her, perfectly unruffled by what he had said, his tawny eyes full of devilment. "Faith, but you intrigue me, Marny Lester," he told her. "Surely there can't be vinegary spinster leanings hidden away under your pretty skin and green eyes?"

She stood on the kerb that faced the square where the Clinic was situated, waiting for an approaching car to go past. She could hear Errol laughing beside her, and suddenly her burst of indignation did seem vinegary and spinsterish. She began to laugh too, gaily and boyishly, and in that moment the car swept past. It was a black Bentley, and as the laughter of the couple on the kerb rang out in that quiet roadway, the driver of the car turned his head and a frown contracted his forehead above light grey eyes. Paul Stillman stared at Marny, with her hair in a tangled cloud above her green laughing eyes and wisps of grass clinging to the white skirt of her dress.

Paul wasn't to know that she had been racing about with a couple of high-spirited youngsters for the best part of the afternoon. To him, as he took a quick glance at her companion, she appeared flushed and dishevelled, after a far from innocent romp in the grass with a man he both distrusted and disliked, but who he kept at the Clinic because he happened to be exceptionally good at his job. If Errol wanted to flirt with the nurses, he was perfectly at liberty to do so, off the Clinic premises, and if the nurses lost their heads, well, that was their business, they were all over twenty-one. But Marny Lester was a different cup of tea. She was parentless and a country girl, and a lot more attractive than she fully realized. Paul felt responsible for her, and as he swung the Bentley into the kerb in front of the Clinic, his lips were hard and compressed. Yes, he felt responsible for her, and he also felt rather disappointed in her.

"This ain't a hospital, is it, Mr. Stillman? Cor, it looks more like something out of the pictures!" exclaimed a young Cockney voice, and in a moment the hard look went from Paul's mouth and he smiled down at the child who occupied the seat beside him.

"I told you my place wasn't like an ordinary hospital, didn't I, Ginger? Now do you feel a bit better about stopping here?" he asked.

The boy nodded as he gazed past Paul's shoulder at the impressive stone steps that led up to the front entrance of the Clinic, where Corinthian pillars gleamed white in the sunshine. He had a pinched little face that made him look a lot younger than his seven years, and his shock of bright red hair seemed to hold all the colour that was missing from his face. His right shoulder was held crookedly and high, and when Paul lifted him from the car, he gazed about him with long-lashed brown eyes. Paul had brought the boy's few bits of clothing from the Orphanage, and he was reaching into the car for the small suitcase they were in, when footsteps approached along the pavement. He glanced up and saw Marny and Errol Dennis. Marny had seen Ginger, who had climbed the Clinic steps and was standing on the top one, and a glad little cry broke from her and she came running towards the car. "Mr. Stillman, they let you bring the boy! Oh, I'm so pleased!" she exclaimed.

But her employer stood regarding her without an answering smile, and she grew perplexed, and rather uncomfortable, as his frosty eyes swept over her. She couldn't imagine what she'd done to make him look at her so disapprovingly, for when they had parted in his office that morning he had been genial to the point of fatherliness. She bit her lip troubledly, and glanced up at the Clinic steps at Ginger, who was watching her with a great deal of interest.

"Hullo, Ginger!" she said.

"Hullo, miss!" He stood on the edge of the step and gave her a grin. "Are you a nurse, miss?"

"No, my name's Marny," she explained. "I'm Mr. Stillman's secretary."

"Oh!" His lip dropped slightly and he glanced down at his shoes. "I thought fer a minute you was a nurse . . . in your white dress an' all." His exceptionally long eyelashes threw shadows on to his pale cheeks, and Marny saw him shiver, as though with cold. She thought of the two vigorous children she had played with in the park, running about with puppyish freedom and red-cheeked with health, and her heart ached for this poor little scrap with the crippled shoulder. She met Paul Stillman's eyes. "Could I take Ginger to his room and help him settle in, Mr. Stillman?" she appealed. "I – I think he'd like me to."

Paul hadn't missed Ginger's instinctive reaching out towards Marny as someone both young and sympathetic, and he couldn't deny her to the boy, despite his feeling that she had rather damaged the estimation he had been forming of her as a level-headed young person, with a fastidious streak. "All right, Marny, you can settle Ginger in if you'd both like that," he agreed. "He's having room twelve on the third floor. He'll be next to Ada Barrington. You haven't met her yet, but she's a great old character. She used to be a very famous music-hall star."

Ada Barrington? The name immediately rang a bell in Mar-

songs her father had taught her, 'Billy, My Big, Big Boy', and ny's mind, and then she thought of one of the old music-hall she remembered that it was Ada Barrington who had made the song famous when her father was a boy and he used to play truant from school to go and sit in the gallery of the old Princess Theatre in Norwich. Her green eyes glistened, but Paul Stillman was plainly in an unsympathetic mood, so she bit back an eager acknowledgement of Ada Barrington's name, accepted the suitcase he held out to her and ran up the steps to Ginger.

"So that's the kid from the Orphanage?" Errol remarked, as Marny took hold of Ginger's hand and they disappeared into the Clinic. Errol glanced back at Paul. "When will you want some pictures of that shoulder?"

"Not yet. We'll let him get used to us, and I want to build him up a bit before attempting any surgery. He's been through the mill, poor little blighter, and his nerves are in a bad state." Then Paul met Errol's eyes and he said, deliberately: "You don't waste much time, do you, Dennis? Saw you coming out of the park with Marny."

"Did you, now?" Errol thought of Marny's tumbled hair, and it amused him, for a very private reason, that Paul Stillman should have jumped to the conclusion he'd been kissing that innocent baby. It was funny, he lazily thought, how laughably blind some very shrewd men could be at times.

"She's a sweet kid," he drawled, "and playful as a kitten." He flicked his cigarette end from his fingers and strolled up the Clinic steps. A smile flickered on his lips as he heard Paul give way to temper and slam the car door.

Ginger's room was bright and airy and it overlooked the Clinic grounds. Ginger had to examine everything – the dressing-table and the wardrobe, the bedside cabinet, and even the rugs on the floor. Marny unpacked his suitcase and laid his clothes away in the drawers of the dressing-table. When she had finished, she sat on the foot of the bed and she and Ginger got really acquainted. Children know instinctively whether the sympathy of adults is genuine or not, and there was no doubt in Ginger's young heart about the sympathy he felt in Marny as she drew him against her.

"I'm going to 'ave an operation," he told her importantly, "on my shoulder." He felt along Marny's shoulder, as if to say that his shoulder, too, would be straight like hers one day. He smiled into her face. "You've got green eyes, miss, just like lime drops."

A smile darted across her face at the description. "You can call me Marny," she told him.

He said the name to himself, and he touched her with wondering hands. She was something very new in his young life, which had only held back-street squalor and brutality, and then the austerity of the Orphanage. He had been about four and a half years old when his mother had left him, and though vague memories of her persisted in his mind, they were memories wholly dissociated from the clean, faintly scented freshness of Marny's skin, the soft feel of her hair, and the gentleness of her voice. Ginger's young mind sought around for an appropriate expression to describe her, and because his only pleasant memories were associated with the cinema, to which a neighbour of his father's used to take him occasionally, to get him out of the way when the drunken Farning brought women home, he said to her: "You're just like someone on the pictures, miss."

"Am I, Ginger?" She didn't make the mistake of laughing at the compliment. "How nice of you to say so."

"Peoples on the pictures live in great big palaces, you know, miss, and they 'ave lots of 'usbands and wives." He gazed at her with solemn, long-lashed eyes. "'Ave you got a 'usband?"

"No, Ginger, I'm not married."

"Don't you want to be?"

"Only if someone very nice will love me very, very much, Ginger, until we're both terribly old and ready to go to heaven."

"Will *he* do that, miss?"

"Who, Ginger?" She looked mystified.

"The laughing man."

"The laughing – oh, I see!" Her arms hugged the boy as she smiled comprehendingly. "That's Mr. Dennis, darling. He works here, but I don't think he could ever love one girl until he's very old." She glanced at her wrist watch. "Your tea will be coming along soon. Are you hungry?"

He nodded, and then, because he had a piece of information to impart that was very hush-hush, he put his lips right against Marny's ear, tickling her as he whispered: "If you like, Marny, I'll marry you when I'm grown up and all well again."

"And does this mean we're engaged?" she whispered back, with appropriate seriousness.

"Yes," he said, and they smiled at one another.

They were eating their tea together at a table in the sunny window embrasure, when Paul Stillman came to see how Ginger was settling in. As he opened the door and his glance settled on Marny and Ginger, busily tucking into banana sandwiches and jam sponge, an involuntary smile came into his eyes.

Ginger turned in his chair and directed a jammy grin at him. "Hullo, Mr. Stillman," he said. "We're 'aving our tea . . . and I don't mind about stopping 'ere now."

Paul strolled to the table, where he helped himself to a banana sandwich. "I'm glad to hear you want to stay, Ginger. I suppose it's my pretty secretary you've got your eye on?"

Ginger nodded solemnly, while Marny blushed as Paul munched his sandwich and looked at her with a cynical expression replacing the smile in his eyes. "You appear to have a way with the boys, Marny," he drawled.

CHAPTER III

MARNY was soon absorbed and deeply interested in her job.

July flowered like a rich blossom, and in her free time from the office she read story books to Ginger in the sunshine of the Clinic grounds and told him about the wild animals and strange birds that frequented the lonely stretches of the Norfolk Broads. He liked to hear about the seaside as well, for he had never seen the sea or played on the sands with a bucket and a spade, and Marny described Yarmouth to him from end to end, telling him how the fine sand blew on the wind and how the big, tossy-ball waves came rolling inshore, shiny with pirates' silver. Ginger had a quick, eager mind and he thoroughly enjoyed Marny's colourful descriptions. One in particular appealed to him, and this referred to Paul Stillman.

He stood talking to them for quite a while one afternoon, and when he was suddenly called away by a nurse, Ginger put his face against Marny's neck and asked her why Mr. Stillman had a big hole in his chin.

Marny's colourful imagination had no difficulty in supplying an explanation, and the cleft in her employer's chin became a secret cave in which lived an enchanted princess the size of a halfpenny. Sometimes on fine days, Marny assured Ginger, she could be seen sitting on a cockle shell combing her long black hair.

When Paul examined the boy he must often have wondered why his chin so obviously fascinated him, and then Ginger confided the story to Ada Barrington, and she thought it so good she passed it on to Paul when he came to massage her back for her one morning.

"I always thought the devil lived there," she guffawed, and Paul paid her back by giving her a nip where she hadn't been nipped for a long while.

"I'm a reformed character now, Ada," he said. "I get married in October."

"October, eh? I suppose your lovely Ilena is having all the trimmings? Bridesmaids? Choirboys? Buckets of champagne?"

"Yeah! I'd have settled for something quicker and less fussy, but Ilena will look like a dream, so I guess I'll bear the agony of striped pants, but I'm damned if I'm going to wear a high hat."

"How's Ilena's young sister getting along?"

"Her wrists have healed, but I think she's got a broken heart, Ada, and I haven't a diploma for mending those."

"They never mend altogether, Paul." Suddenly there was a more sober note in Ada Barrington's voice. "No, they never really mend, though they can be patched up like dropped vases, and if you don't stand too close to them, or expect them to take too much rough handling, then they pass for hearts."

"You sound as though you're speaking from experience, Ada."

"I lost a good man out in Jo'burg forty years ago and I've never quite got over him. Ah, that feels better, Paul. Much easier." She was a big woman, but he lifted her and resettled her among the bedcovers without effort, and as she straightened the straps of her nightdress, her gay old eyes twinkled up at him. His unruly lock of hair had fallen on to his forehead and the sleeves of his white shirt were rolled above his elbows, showing dark-haired, vigorous forearms. He looked all man, she thought, with appreciation. All man and a good-hearted one. She inclined her head towards the room next door. "The little

49

chap is being X-rayed this morning, isn't he, Paul?"

He nodded, thrusting the dark hair back off his forehead. "It makes your blood run cold when you think of the heartless way some folks treat their children, doesn't it? The law's too damn lenient with them, and though people like myself can sometimes remedy the physical damage caused by these inhuman brutes, we can't do much about the mental scars that are left. I hope to put Ginger's body right for him, but he'll probably be subject to nervous fears for the rest of his life."

"Poor little lamb!" Ada's earring, pendant and studded with real diamonds, shook with feeling. Ada was never without her earrings, even in bed, and her bold, still handsome face was always heavily powdered and rouged. She looked an actress, and at seventy-six she still had the resonant voice of one and a gay, slightly salacious twinkle in her blue eyes. Paul liked her very much. Most of her old friends had gradually slipped away out of her life, leaving her rather lonely, and he believed it was company she sought at the Clinic as much as bodily relief. She was inclined to be arthritic and she came to the Clinic about twice a year. He always kept a bed for her, despite the fact that there wasn't very much he could do for her particular complaint.

She watched him roll down his sleeves. "Do you ever think about going back to Canada?" she asked.

"Drew, my brother, would like me to go back, but I'm kinda settled here now I've got this place going. And I don't think Ilena would really like living there." He smiled as he swung into his jacket. "There are only three civilized places for Ilena – London, Paris and Rome. I don't think I dare take her too far away from her beloved Paris fashion shows, Ada." His voice held a sardonic note, but there was an indulgent curve to his mouth, and Ada supposed that a gorgeous armful like Ilena Justine had to be excused her predilections for fashionable society, lovely clothes and a much less responsible approach to life than her husband-to-be. Responsible he might be, but he was also possessed of a vigour that was never fully impaired, even at the end of a long day, and Ada wasn't really surprised that he felt the need of an exciting partner rather than a domesticated one. Ilena Justine was exciting all right. She had an exquisite body and her mouth always looked as though it was waiting to be hungrily kissed.

"Well, I've got to love you and leave you, Ada. I'm always up and down like Barney's bull on a Thursday, and Marny's waiting to do the staff wages with me." Paul broke into a laugh and fingered his clefted chin. "Funny kid, isn't she?" he murmured.

He hurried downstairs. Ilena and he were dining at the French Embassy that evening and he wanted to get Thursday's usual pile of paper work off his hands as soon as possible. The Embassy dinner was rather an important affair, and Ilena had actually managed to arouse Nadia's interest in the frock she was wearing and she was coming over to the Clinic that evening to show it to her cousin.

The nurses' bungalow was so placed that its attractive verandah caught the last rays of the setting sun of an evening. They gilded the framework of the verandah, spilling upon Marny as she rested against the wooden rail, and softening Julie Brelson's bleached hair to gold. Julie lounged in a basket-chair, manicuring her fingernails. "The rich have all the fun, don't they?" she said, in a slightly disgruntled tone of voice.

"You say that, Julie, but I bet you wouldn't change places with Nadia Justine," Marny replied. "Money can't seem to buy back her good health, and you are able to go dancing and to do a dozen and one things she's barred from doing."

51

Julie prodded at an obstinate half-moon with a little orange stick. "I wonder what will happen about that French chap of hers? If he's found guilty they'll send him to prison for years, won't they?"

"I didn't know you could read French," Marny said, sharply.

"Oh, I was friendly with a French nurse during my time at Barts and she taught me some. I'm no brilliant scholar at it, mind, but I get by." Then Julie glanced up, and when she saw the frowning way Marny was regarding her, a wave of give-away colour swept over her pert face. "You're a bit too blasted quick on the uptake, you are!" she muttered. "You've guessed it was me who brought that paper in to Nadia, haven't you?"

"Why on earth did you do it, Julie?"

"Well, she kept on asking and I felt sorry for her. She'd al-ready guessed there was something in the wind from remarks he'd let drop in his letters, but I didn't think for a minute she'd try and do away with herself when she read that he'd been ar-rested and was being sent for trial. Good grief, I nearly died of fright when I took her tea in that afternoon and found her with her wrists all slashed open. Turned me real sick, it did."

"You posted her letters to him as well, I suppose?"

"Well, I didn't see any harm in it, Marny. I just thought old Justine was against her friendship with René Blanchard be-cause of the way she is." Julie shrugged. "Some fathers are a bit funny about that sort of thing, though she's perfectly all right, apart from not being able to walk. She could get married if she wanted to." Julie fiddled with some of the manicuring para-phernalia on a table beside her. "You won't tell Mr. Stillman I posted those letters and brought papers in for her, will you, Marny?"

"Of course not!" Marny said at once. "What do you take me for?"

Julie didn't answer right away, and the sweet smell of nail varnish drifted across the verandah as she began to paint her nails. "The boss would give me the push right away if he found out, and you seem pretty thick with him." Julie glanced up and her rather shallow blue eyes searched Marny's face. "Nadia gave me a couple of quid, you see, and it's one of the rules here that we're not to take money from the patients, so promise me on your oath you'll keep all this under your hat. I don't want to lose this job."

"Naturally I shan't say anything, but I do think you might have had a bit more sense." Marny turned and gazed out over the Clinic grounds and the trees rustled gently in the evening air. "Ilena's coming to the Clinic tonight to show her dance frock to Nadia. I wonder what it's like?"

"Pretty fabulous, you bet," Julie replied. "The Justines are rolling in cash, and I'd have thought she'd have wanted to marry someone in the upper set. Mr. Stillman's attractive, of course, but I've heard he's invested most of his money in this place, and if it ever goes crash, he'll go crash with it." Julie held out a hand and fluttered her fingernails in the air to dry them. "Um, the boss isn't bad, in his cave-man fashion, but Errol Dennis is my idea of a good-looking man."

"Errol Dennis is a bit too good-looking, and he knows it," Marny laughed.

Julie frowned slightly at this remark and her eyes slipped over Marny, who looked very fresh and slender in a slim-fitting black skirt and a white blouse with Paisley-patterned collar and cuffs. "Has Errol been giving you the glad-eye, Marny?" Julie asked, in a stiff voice.

"He has done so, a couple of times," Marny admitted. "He's asked me to go to a rather grand dance with him on the twenty-fourth of August."

"The Chardmore Charity Ball?" Julie demanded sharply. "The one the Chardmores throw every year to help medical research."

"That's right." Marny swung round from the verandah rail, and the light that was spilling out through the bungalow windows showed her the white, jealous sharpness of Julie's face. Then Julie jumped to her feet and orange-sticks and pieces of cotton-wool rained out of her lap. "Are you going with him?" she demanded.

"I had thought of going." Marny frowned as she took note of Julie's agitation. "I'm fond of dancing, but if he's promised to take you—"

"He hasn't promised," Julie admitted sullenly. "He's hinted once or twice that he might take me, and — and I'd give anything to go. It's one of the biggest dances of the year. They hold it in the grounds of Lord Chardmore's house at Teddington and everybody wears a fancy costume and a mask." A definite suggestion of tears shimmered in Julie's eyes. "*You* could afford to buy your own ticket. We all know you're only working for the fun of it."

Which was true, Marny supposed, while the thought flashed across her mind that Errol Dennis was as careless with people's feelings as a child with a bag of marbles. He had no right to half-promise one girl he'd take her to the Chardmore Ball and then carelessly switch to another one. No wonder poor Julie looked on the verge of tears. Marny ran across the verandah to her and gave her a quick reassuring hug. "Don't worry," she said, "I will buy my own ticket, and that handsome devil shall take the pair of us. I didn't know it was a costume dance. It'll be fun, Julie, dreaming up a pair of really original costumes."

Marny's warm eagerness of heart was not to be resisted, and Julie returned her smile. "You'd really buy another ticket?"

she asked.

"Certainly. Errol seems to like playing the sheik, so he can saunter into the Chardmore house with a girl on each arm."

Julie gazed back at Marny with rather astounded eyes. "Most girls are a bit dazzled by Errol, but you're ever so cool about him, Marny. Don't you – don't you like him?"

"He's all right," Marny replied, after a bit of thought. "He can be quite nice when he likes."

"I like him," Julie admitted. "I've been out with him several times, and he goes to ever such swell places in the West End. I don't really know how he can afford to go to them. He gets a good salary here, it's true, but it hardly runs to the Carlton Grill after he's paid the rent of his flat and bought his clothes and his meals. D'you know what, Marny, I believe he plays chemmy."

"Chemmy?" Marny looked mystified.

"Chemin-de-fer. If you're lucky you can win quite a bit at it."

"What makes you think he plays it?" Marny queried, with interest and hardly any surprise. She didn't think very much would surprise her where Errol Dennis was concerned.

"Well," Julie said, "I was out dancing with him once, at a club where he goes, and a tall chap put a hand on his shoulder and said he was trying to get some of Errol's luck to rub on him. Errol just laughed, but I knew the other man was talking about gambling. He looked the reckless-eyed sort you'd expect to see at the chemmy clubs, and Errol must get his money from somewhere." Julie bent down and collected together the or-ange-stick and pieces of cotton wool she had dropped. Her voice came rather muffledly as she went on: "That man said something else, Marny. He looked at me and then he asked Errol where his *other* girl-friend was. He winked – you know, the way men do when they're talking about someone awfully glamorous. But Errol got annoyed. He stopped laughing and he danced me away ever so quickly."

Julie straightened up. "I – I know he plays around, but I can't help the way I feel about him. He can be ever so sweet at times."

And Marny knew this to be true. Little Ginger had been terribly nervous about having his X-rays taken, but Errol had anticipated this and brought a cowboy hat to wear in the X-ray room. Ginger had a passion for playing cowboys and he had been thrilled by the hat, and the X-ray pictures had been taken without fuss or nerves.

Errol Dennis was an enigma, Marny decided. You couldn't approve of him, and yet you couldn't entirely disapprove, but any girl who let herself fall in love with him was asking for heartache.

Julie packed her varnishes and orange-sticks back into her manicure box, and she and Marny walked into the nurses' sitting-room, where one of the nurses immediately glanced up from her knitting and announced that the television set had gone on strike.

"Liven us up, Marny," she begged. "Give us a tune on the piano. Old Green, over in number ten, has given me the blues with that knee of his. I feel sorry for the poor old boy, but he does carry on. While Mr. Gordon was seeing to him, he gave me an awful wallop on the chest. We should get danger money in this business."

"Didn't Alec Gordon offer to rub the place and make it better?" Julie laughed, as she helped Marny to clear some underwear and a couple of starched caps off the piano. Marny had been delighted to find the bungalow equipped with a piano.

"Are you kidding?" The other nurse wore a grin as she

counted stitches. "Life is real, life is earnest for our Alec. The only elevations he's interested in are knee-caps and ankle-bones."

Marny smiled to herself as her hands wandered over the piano keyboard. Alec Gordon was so shy, he seemed to wear a permanent blush, and the nurses just wouldn't leave him alone.

"That's nice, Marny," Nurse Donkin said. "What is it?"

"An Irish ballad my mother taught me," and Marny was suddenly so absorbed in the music that she didn't notice the renewed jealousy of Julie Brelson's glance. The lovely Irish melody stole from under her fingers and drifted its way out of the bungalow and across the quiet, evening-wrapped grounds to the Clinic.

Ilena had not yet arrived, and Paul was waiting for her in Nadia's room. He looked very tall and rather aloof in evening wear and his unruly hair had been drilled into an immaculate tidiness for once.

"You look every bit the distinguished osteopath this even-ing, Paul," Nadia remarked, and then she turned her head to-wards the half-opened window, where the curtains stirred gently in the warm air. "*Who* is that who plays the piano?" she asked. "Several times I have lain here and been treated to a free concert."

"The music doesn't disturb you, does it, Nadia?" he asked at once.

She shook her head, and Paul walked to the window, where the midsummer sky still held little shimmers of daylight and a breath of night-scented stock stole past his cheek. The music Marny played was not familiar to him, but it had the unmistak-able fey quality of Ireland and it cast a spell as it wandered among the shadows, down there in the grounds.

"It's my new secretary, Nadia," he explained. "She plays
57

very well, doesn't she? Her mother was Mary Farrel, the concert pianist."

"Was she? How interesting." But there was no real interest in Nadia's voice and Paul sighed quietly as he walked back to the bed. He watched Nadia's pale face, with the strange, tilted eyes that held so much unhappiness. He remembered how she had fought him the afternoon she had tried to die; now her eyes were hopeless and resigned. Resigned to a life without purpose, a life without René Blanchard.

"Nadia —"

"No, Paul, don't talk to me about what might be done for me if only I would be confident. I am an empty shell. At nineteen I am an empty, purposeless thing, created only to lie like a log and count the empty minutes as they go by. I accept it! Let it be as it is!"

He took hold of her hands and pressed them. They were cold, lax, like dead hands, and he thought of the alive vibrancy of Marny Lester's, stealing over those piano keys with an inborn knowledge and power. He glanced back towards the window and Nadia's dark eyes followed his glance.

"Do you like your new secretary, Paul?" she asked.

"Yes, she's a capable kid. I don't know what I'd do without her in the office now."

"She is pretty, I am told."

He nodded. Then, very casually, he said: "Would you care to meet her, Nadia. She's your own age, you know."

"What, she is a hundred years old?" Nadia broke into laughter that was awful to listen to, for it had no youth, no hope in it. "Oh, Paul, what would your pretty secretary talk to me about? Her gay outings? Her many boy-friends? Her wonderful, untroubled future, spent in the arms of an adoring husband?"

"I don't think so, Nadia."

"What, she is pretty and has no boy-friends?"

"She may have." He frowned as he thought of Errol Dennis. "I don't probe into her private affairs, but it did occur to me that you and she might have a mutual interest in music. As you can hear, she's a very talented little pianist."

But Nadia turned her head restlessly on her pillows. "I'm not good company for anyone, Paul. I am a ghost. I would frighten her."

He laughed a little. "I don't think Marny's easily frightened, my dear. See her for a little while tomorrow. It will buck you up to have company."

But before Nadia could give him a definite answer, the bedroom door opened and Ilena walked in. She was wrapped round in a really lovely white silk cloak, exactly like a Bedouin Arab, and diamonds flamed and gleamed in her tiny ears. She loved making a dramatic entrance, and her petrol-blue eyes danced with gaiety as they met Paul's. *"Chéri*, how distinguished you look!" She ran to him and held up her mouth for a quick kiss, and he smilingly obliged. Then she turned to the bed. "And how is my Nadia tonight?" she asked.

"I'm all right, Ilena. I like your cloak."

"Wonderful, isn't?" Ilena laughed excitedly and ran a jewelled hand down the silk.

"Ilena, for heaven's sake relieve the tension and let us see what you've got on underneath it," Paul ordered.

The silk fell open with a rustling sound and Paul caught his breath, audibly. Ilena wore clinging carnation red and her arms and shoulders showed startlingly white.

Nadia's eyes moved over her cousin. "You look wonderful, Ilena," she said, "but you are showing an immodest amount of bosom."

59

"I'll say you are, honey!" Paul's left eyebrow described a quizzical arch as he stood regarding his fiancée. "Couldn't you hitch the thing up a bit. I shall be in a sweat all night, expecting it to fall down round your waist just as the Ambassador is proposing a toast."

"Don't be nonsensical, daarling!" She fluttered her lashes at him. "It is the style and it cannot fall down. There are tiny bones holding it to me. Here, feel me." She took his hands and pressed them to the lovely, moulding silk. "There you are, you silly man. I am quite safe."

The fragrant expensiveness of her perfume drifted to him and her feminine warmth flowed into his fingers and along his veins, and suddenly he wanted very much to be alone with her. Their evenings together always seemed full of other people. If they went to a theatre a party of friends invariably accompanied them. And they couldn't walk into a restaurant without Ilena spotting someone she knew, and that someone always had to come over and dine with them. Tonight they would sit apart at the Embassy dining-table and probably have no more than a couple of dances together.

"Honey, do we have to go to this Embassy turn-out?" he asked. "I'd settle for a quiet drive out to the Surrey Windmill. They do an awfully nice meal there –"

"Of course we must go, Paul!" Ilena's eyes looked quite shocked. "I ordered this frock especially, and several of my friends from Paris will be there. Line Cabot will have lots of news for me –"

"Yes," Nadia broke in, "she will be able to tell you whether they are going to shoot René or leave him to rot his life away in a prison cell."

Paul winced and Ilena went running to the bed. She caught Nadia against her rustling silk and scented flesh, and extrava-

60

gant Gallic endearments spilled from her. Nadia suffered them for a moment only. Tiredly she withdrew from her cousin's arms. "You will be late at the Embassy," she said.

"*Chéri*," Ilena brushed at her cousin's dark hair, "is René worth all this unhappiness?"

"Oh, leave me alone, Ilena." Nadia turned her face into her pillows. "Go to your dance, please."

"Yes, come along." Paul walked Ilena to the door.

"But we cannot leave her like this!" she protested. "She might hurt herself again!"

"I'm not leaving her," he replied. "I'm going to get somebody to sit with her. She had a sedative earlier on, so she should sleep in a while."

When they reached the office, he took up the phone and buzzed the nurses' bungalow. Scotty was off duty this evening, but she wouldn't mind sparing half an hour to sit with Nadia. He didn't think the girl would attempt suicide again, but he wasn't taking any chances. Someone came on the line and he asked for Scotty.

"I'm sorry, Mr. Stillman, but Nurse Truscott and several of the other nurses have gone to see a film at the Dominion."

He recognized Marny's voice, and after a momentary hesitation he asked her if she could spare half an hour herself to sit with Nadia.

"I'll come over right away," she said, and he replaced the receiver with a feeling of relief.

"Your secretary is unusually obliging, Paul." Ilena took out a powder compact and studied her mouth, but the kiss he had given her up in Nadia's room had not disturbed her lipstick. "Are you training her to be a nurse?"

He frowned at the slightly malicious edge to Ilena's voice. "It's damned good of Marny to volunteer to sit with Nadia," he snapped. "She's been pounding a typewriter all the afternoon, and that's a bit more tiring than sitting in a beauty salon having your face massaged, which I don't doubt is where you've been."

"Don't be sarcastic." Ilena glared at him. "You are showing off like a spoiled boy because I won't drive to that bourgeois Windmill place you are so fond of. I don't care to have spiders dropping down my neck while I eat my dinner under a tree. I haven't forgotten the last time. I know you thought it a big joke when that huge striped thing dropped on to my shoulder."

A smile sprang to his mouth at the memory of her extravagant horror. "Ilena, it was rather funny. You behaved just as though some enormous tarantula had got hold of you, instead of a tiny English garden spider." He stepped forward to take hold of her hands, but she turned away from him pettishly, and his frown came back.

"Is it so wrong that I should want you to myself now and again?" he demanded. "I'm a man, Ilena, not a pet dog on a lead. Just lately you seem to be forgetting the fact." And, goaded by this fit of sulks she had developed and the way the carnation red silk clung to the curves of her body, he swung her savagely against his chest and took her wilful scarlet mouth in a long, hard kiss. When he let her go, her lipstick was decidedly disturbed this time and Marny was tapping rather self-consciously at the half-open door.

Paul took out a handkerchief and wiped Ilena's lipstick from his mouth in a perfectly unembarrassed manner. "I shan't be long, Ilena," he said. "I'll just take Marny up to Nadia's room."

Ilena was fuming. He had crushed her frock and she would have to repaint her mouth. "You boor!" she cried out, disregarding Marny's startled presence. "I will not be treated like a – a tart!"

"Then you shouldn't dress like one," he retorted coolly, but his eyes were dangerous in their lightness as they met Marny's . . . like silver flashing on the edge of a rapier, she thought. "Come along!" he marched Marny across the hall and up the stairs. He explained that Nadia was feeling depressed and that it would ease his mind if someone sat with her until she fell asleep.

"You don't feel nervous about sitting with her?" He faced Marny in the dim corridor, and when she shook her head, his hands found her shoulders, slight and delicately-boned under her white blouse. "You're a good kid, Marny," he murmured. "I'm beginning to depend on you quite a lot, aren't I?"

"I like knowing I'm of use, Mr. Stillman." Her smile, however, was hesitant. There had been something ugly about that scene downstairs, and she could feel a troubling urgency in Paul's hands upon her shoulders. She felt that he wanted to be comforted in some way, but he wasn't – well, he wasn't Ginger. She couldn't wrap her arms round him and tell him a fairy story.

"You're proving of great use, Marny, in the office and where little Ginger is concerned," he said. "I'd rather like to apologize for the doubts I had when you first came here."

"I knew you had doubts, Mr. Stillman." She hesitated a moment, and in the dimness of the corridor he saw an enquiring expression come into her green eyes. "What did I do to annoy you so much on my second day here? I – I couldn't think what I'd done –"

She felt his hands tighten on her shoulders and a smile that was rather cynical flickered on the edge of his mouth. "To tell you the truth, Marny, I saw you coming out of Regent's Park with Errol Dennis. Naturally it isn't any of my business what my employees do in their off-duty time, but I do happen to

63

know he's a bit of a philanderer, and you'd assured me, earlier on that day, that you had every intention of steering clear of him." That cynical smile flickered again on Paul's lips. "One look at you, Marny, was enough to tell me you hadn't been in the park discussing the weather with Errol."

"Oh!" Comprehension flashed into her eyes, and indignation quickly followed it. "I looked untidy, and you thought — you thought he'd been kissing me? But it isn't true! I was playing with a couple of boys and their kite. We almost lost it and Errol came along and — and rescued it. The boys wanted him to show them how to fly the kite properly, and I got untidy racing about the grass —"

She broke off, for suddenly, quite unexpectedly, Paul gave a low, rather boyish laugh and caught her against him in a contrite hug. "Damn my low mind!" he exclaimed. "I might have guessed you were on the level and not to be easily won over by Dennis's sort."

She laughed a little herself, glad the misunderstanding was cleared up. It was true she had agreed to go to the Chardmore Ball with Errol, but only because half the Clinic staff were going as well.

"Am I forgiven?" She felt Paul's hands slip down her bare arms.

"Of course."

"You nice child." Then he swung open the door of Nadia's room. "It's me again, Nadia," he announced. "I've brought Marny to sit with you for a while." He still held one of Marny's hands and he drew her to the bed, where Nadia's eyes took her in from head to toe.

"Yes, you are very pretty," she said, and her tilted eyes dwelt on the warm vibrancy of Marny's hair. Dwelt sadly, wistfully.

"Thank you, Nadia." Marny sat down in a chair beside the

bed, while Paul took a quick glance at his wrist watch. "Say, I'd better be off!" He shared a smile between the two girls. "I'll see you both in the morning." The door shut behind him and Nadia smiled wearily into Marny's eyes.

"Have you been put in here to guard me, in case I do this again?" She turned her wrists towards Marny and showed her the red scars that marred them. "Trying to die hurt me too much, for that man who has just gone out of that door is a demon. Oh yes!" as Marny's eyes looked startled. "He snatched me back from peace. He swore at me when I begged him to let me go. Then, in case I should still elude him, he sat where you are sitting, all night, like some fierce satanic angel, and defied me to get away from him."

Marny ran gentle fingers over the scars upon the upturned wrists. "One day these will hardly show," she said.

"You know all about my René, I suppose?" Nadia murmured.

"Yes."

"They will shut him away. To imprison him would be imprisoning a wild bird. All beings must be free for René, but he has misguidedly given his support to young hotheads who want to set the world to rights by violent means. He has done wrong, but we only really love someone when we love the bad in them as well as the good, and I cannot put him out of my heart. I have tried. I tried to do it by dying, for while I live I must love him."

"But you're still very young, Nadia —"

"You think that at nineteen one cannot love with the whole of one's being, *chérie*?" Nadia asked. "I loved René when I was a child, back in Provence. It made no difference that he never noticed me. He knew nothing of the way I felt about him, for he was like a god to me and far out of my reach. And then I

65

had my accident and the specialists said I would never dance again. René came to me and said he loved me. Last year he asked Papa if he would let us become betrothed, but Papa said no. He said he would never consent. Never! Never!"

Nadia sighed, and shadows lay under her high cheekbones. "I know, now, why my father disliked René so much, and I can forgive him his dislike, but I – I have no way of stopping my hopeless longing for René. It might be different if I were not crippled."

"Are you crippled, Nadia?" Marny asked, quietly.

"Look!" Nadia pummelled her unmoving legs. "Look! Once my legs could carry me across a stage like a bird, now they are useless. I know they are. I have known since the night I had my accident. I heard them say it as I was carried to my dressing-room. She will never dance again, they said."

"She will never dance again!"

Those poignant words stayed in Marny's mind long after Nadia had fallen fast asleep and she was tucked up in her own bed, back at the bungalow.

In those words, she realized, lay the barrier that was keeping Paul Stillman from reaching Nadia. Nadia couldn't face knowing that though he might make her walk again, he could never give her back her dancing feet. The dancing feet that might have helped her to forget the man she loved, the man she might soon lose for ever.

Marny and Nadia soon became very good friends. The weather continued fine and Marny got into the habit of taking Nadia out in her invalid chair while Ginger was having his afternoon nap. Paul was usually busy with his patients most afternoons, and Nadia discovered that she welcomed the outings. Marny always had plenty to talk about, and with each passing hour, now, being alone with her thoughts was becoming more and more intolerable for the French girl. Marny knew this and she always tried to have a topic of conversation that would successfully divert Nadia's thoughts from René Blanchard, if only for half an hour.

They were enjoying the sunshine in Regent's Park one Wednesday afternoon when it occurred to her to ask Nadia's advice on a costume for the Chardmore Ball. Lady Chardmore had decided that it would be an exciting idea if everybody attending the Ball this year came as a forest creature or a plant, anything, in fact, which might reasonably be found in a forest. Julie Brelson had decided to go as a waterfall. She intended to wear a turquoise-blue dress and to let her fair hair rain on to her shoulders. Marny couldn't make up her mind what to go as.

"Why not go as a dragonfly?" Nadia glanced round at Marny and smiled. "With your long hair, *chérie*, and your green eyes, you should make a most *petite* dragonfly."

"H'm, it's an idea." Marny was immediately intrigued. "I wonder where I'd be able to hire such a costume?"

"I happen to have a delightful dragonfly outfit stored among my ballet costumes at Ilena's flat," Nadia said. "You can borrow that."

"Can I really?" Marny looked delighted. "What's it like, Nadia? Describe it to me."

Nadia proceeded to do so. It had glittering wings attached to the bodice and it was worn with emerald-green tights and a skull-cap set with tiny red globes that flickered on and off like eyes. "You will probably have to renew the battery that works the little globes, *chérie*," she added, "for the costume has lain untouched in my trunk for the past two years."

"It sounds lovely, and you are a dear to want to lend it to me!" Marny bent over Nadia and gave her a grateful hug. "I promise I shan't damage it in any way. I'm only sorry I've got to wait until next Monday before I can go and collect it. Your sister doesn't return from Paris until then, does she?" Ilena, so Paul had informed Marny, had gone over to Paris to see about her trousseau.

"But I have a door-key," Nadia said at once. "You could go over to the flat before Monday. My costume trunk is kept in a cupboard in the hallway, so you would have no trouble finding it. And the key to the trunk is always kept in the lock."

Marny, however, looked doubtful. "I don't much like the idea of going to Ilena's flat while she's away, Nadia."

"Don't be silly, *chérie*. It is my flat as well, and we must ascertain whether or not the costume needs any alterations. I was but seventeen when I wore it last and it may have to be let out a little." Her eyes measured Marny. "I was very thin, and I think you have a little more bosom than I had at that time."

"Well, all right, if you're sure Ilena won't be annoyed. I'll pop over during the weekend. I shan't be able to go before then. Tomorrow's our busy day in the office and Mr. Stillman wants me to renew the filing cards on Friday. Some of them are a bit dog-eared."

They were passing a daisy bush and Nadia plucked one of the tiny white flowers. "Do you like working for Paul?" she asked.

"Very much." Marny's voice was warmer than she knew, and Nadia turned and looked at her, really looked at her, seeing her vibrant attractiveness and the warm promise of her smiling mouth. "You never talk of a beau, Marny," she said. "Do men not interest you?"

"I – don't think about them a terrible lot, Nadia." Marny grinned. "Perhaps I'm the spinster type."

Nadia laughed and shook her head with Gallic incredibility.

"*Allez-vous-en!* It is that you will want a real man – no *homme de paille* will satisfy you, *chérie*." She stroked her cheek with the tiny, soft daisy. René came into her mind, and to stop the thought she said quickly: "Paul is very nice, when he isn't pulling my legs this way and that way. He knows I shall never stand upon my feet again."

"He knows nothing of the sort, Nadia," Marny protested. "He's convinced that it's within your power not only to stand upon your feet again, but to walk. I – I think you owe it to him to try, you know."

A flash of anger went across Nadia's face and for a moment she had a fleeting resemblance to Ilena. "He discusses me, I see, like – like some laboratory guinea-pig!"

"Naturally he talks about you, Nadia," Marny admitted. "He wants to help you so much. He believes that it isn't your legs which are fixed and immovable, but your mind. He says while you continue *not* to want to walk, you never will."

"He thinks I *choose* this helplessness? He thinks I am play-acting?" Tears sprang into Nadia's tilted eyes. "*Ma chère*, do you believe this?"

"I don't believe you're consciously choosing to remain helpless, Nadia. Of course I don't. But it seems to me that you don't want to walk because it will mean facing up to the fact that your dancing career is over."

"Everything is over." Nadia stared through her tears at the sunshine over the park. She watched the children skipping along beside their mothers and she saw plump birds perched on the branches of the trees. Then everything swam away out of sight and she was drowning in a hundred memories of long ago, when the world had seemed to hold so much promise. When somewhere deep down in her heart she had known that the tall man with the sun-bronzed face would come to her, put his arms around her and talk of love. . . .

"Take me back to the Clinic!" She swung her chair round so frenziedly she almost knocked Marny off the pathway. "Take me back! Hurry! Hurry! I cannot bear it here a moment longer!"

Marny pushed the chair back towards the square where the Clinic was, and Nadia stared ahead of her, frozen and hopeless. She wouldn't answer Marny when she spoke to her and Marny began to feel tearful herself. She hadn't meant to upset Nadia. The last thing in the world she had wanted was to hurt someone who had already suffered horrible injury to her body and her heart. Uncle Richard always declared that she had a reckless tongue, and it was true! Oh, how could she have said that, about Nadia's dancing career being over? How could she have said it?

She wheeled Nadia out of the park towards the roadway, too miserable to remember that a little extra caution was necessary when crossing this road. It wasn't a main road, therefore traffic had a way of sweeping round from the square with careless speed at times.

This happened today. Marny had pushed Nadia's chair to the middle of the road when a scarlet two-seater suddenly roared round the corner from the direction of the Clinic. Marny saw the car careering down upon her and Nadia a moment before she summoned her wits together and gave Nadia's chair a terrific push towards the safety of the kerb. The next instant she heard the scream of brakes, then one of the car's headlamps punched into her like a spiteful fist and sent her spinning. She cried out with pain and fright as she fell to the road and sharp gravel tore into one of her legs.

She didn't quite pass out, for she was confusedly aware that it was Errol Dennis's voice that spoke to her. Then she felt his

70

arms gather her up off the ground. She lay against his shoulder and she saw in a muzzy kind of way that he had gone very white. "Is Nadia all right?" she asked shakily.

"Let me put you in the car, then I'll go and see." He lowered her to one of the seats, and after that everything began to go dark and a feeling of acute nausea took possession for Marny. She struggled against it, because she had to know that Nadia was all right. She had been in her charge, and Paul Stillman would never forgive her if anything had happened to Nadia. . . .

CHAPTER IV

MARNY was still saying Nadia's name when she regained consciousness and found herself in the surgery of the Clinic. Paul Stillman was bending over her, applying something that stung a little to one of her legs. "Lie still, honey," he murmured. "Nadia's quite safe and sound."

"She isn't hurt? Y-you'd tell me?"

"Sure Mr. Stillman would tell you, dear." Marny saw Nurse Truscott's homely, reassuring face above her. "The poor girl was spilled out of her chair as it hit the kerb, but she's none the worse for that. She even managed to drag herself back into her chair, she was so blamed worried about how you were."

Marny could have cried with thankful relief. "I was so afraid she'd been hurt."

"You're the one who's taken the knocks," Nurse Truscott replied. "Mr. Stillman's had to remove some spiteful bits of gravel from your leg."

Marny could now feel Paul's hands on her right thigh and she gave a jump as something stung her again. "It's only iodine," he said. "Does it sting?"

"Just a little." She lifted her head so that she could see what he was doing. She was stretched on one of the treatment couches, her dress was ripped open to her waist and there were some bright smears of blood on her white slip. She gave a nauseated shudder and sank down again. "Mr. Stillman, it wasn't Errol's fault," she said. "I'm usually careful about that road, especially when I'm with Nadia, but today – I – I just walked across without taking a bit of care." She swallowed dryly.

"Scotty, could I have a drink of water?" she asked.

"Get her a tot of brandy, Scotty," Paul said. "You'll find a bottle in my sitting-room." Nurse Truscott hurried from the surgery and Paul carefully rolled Marny on to her side so that he could examine her right hip. It was badly bruised, but his hands could feel no damage to the bone. The pelvic area was also quite intact, and he shot a relieved smile at her. "You're going to ache a bit, honey, but you've no broken bones. And these gravel scratches should heal in a day or two."

He worked over her for a few more minutes, then at last he came to the head of the couch and adjusted it to a sitting position for her, his arm feeling warm and strong at the back of her shoulders as he lifted her. His face was close to hers for a moment, very definite and masculine with its cleft chin and slashing brows above the luminous grey eyes. "Do you always put other people's welfare before your own?" he murmured.

Her eyes questioned his and he gently stroked the tumbled hair back off her forehead. "You could have been killed, you know. Nadia told me you pushed her chair to safety and left yourself right in the path of that damn car of Dennis's."

"Well, I was in charge of her . . ."

Then her words petered out, for Paul broke into a smile and dropped a soft kiss on the very tip of her nose. "That, Marny, is 'thank you' from Nadia and me," he said. "Now I'd better go and tell Errol Dennis you've no broken bones. I left him pacing about in the hall."

Nurse Truscott reappeared with a bottle and a glass a minute or so after Paul left the surgery. She poured Marny a tot of the brandy and it brought a tinge of colour back into her cheeks. "Oh, Scotty, you don't know what a relief it is, hearing that Nadia's all right," Marny smiled shakily. "Did she really manage to get back into her chair without any help?"

"She certainly did. I'd say that's a good sign, wouldn't you? It proves her legs aren't completely helpless, but then Mr. Stillman has always said that." They were still discussing Nadia and her prospective chances of walking when Paul returned to the surgery. His face was impassive, but his eyes had the tempered brightness of steel; a clear sign that he'd just indulged in an argument. He held up a restraining hand as Marny went to speak.

"It's all very well for you to say this accident was your fault, Marny," he said, "but I've seen Dennis tearing round that corner by the park. He tears round it as though he's taking part in the Monte Carlo rally. Anyway, this has shaken him, and he's gone home with his tail between his legs."

Marny couldn't help feeling rather sorry for Errol, but she saw that Paul wouldn't be argued with on the point. He had made up his mind to lay the bigger share of blame at Errol's door, and she, to tell the truth, was still feeling too shaken up for arguments. Her leg was scraped and sore and her hip continued to throb in a rather sickening way, despite the emollient Paul had applied to the bruise.

She climbed out of bed the following morning like an old lady, but she insisted upon working as it was Thursday and there was a lot of office work to get through, but when their eleven o'clock coffee was brought in Paul suggested they drink it in his sitting-room.

He picked up the tray and carried it towards the door that separated the office from his private quarters. "Come along," he said, "you're looking a bit fragile this morning, Marny, and I feel like making a fuss of you."

She smiled and followed him into his sitting-room, where he proceeded to wait on her for a change. He took a bottle of whisky off the sideboard and poured a finger into each cup of coffee, then he topped up the cups with cream. "Irish coffee," he said, handing her a cup. "It's a good pick-you-up."

"Thank you." While she sipped her coffee, which tasted really good, she frankly examined his sitting-room. It was essentially a man's room, but everything blended most pleasantly, the colours in a raw, striking Van Gogh above the fireplace being echoed in the great cobblestone rug that lay over the floor. The deep chairs were upholstered in natural hide, and Marny was fascinated by the ledge along the back of the big couch, presumably for holding books, ashtrays and glasses.

"Do you like my room, Marny?" Paul sat on the arm of one of the big chairs, and Tiger, his tabby cat, awoke from a doze and climbed on to his knee. Tiger's deep purring mingled with the soft ticking of a clock on the mantelpiece, and Marny sank back in her chair and felt her aching body grow a little easier. "I love it," she replied. She pointed to the painting above the fireplace. "That's a Van Gogh, isn't it, Mr. Stillman? It's so alive with colour. I can almost feel the heat coming off that vivid splash of sunshine."

Paul studied the painting while Tiger sat and enjoyed the feel of the slender, mobile fingers upon his fur. "Colour expressed passion for Van Gogh, sunshine the life-giving element in passion," Paul murmured. "The two were indivisible for him, as they should be, but not everybody belongs to his school of thought." Now the grey eyes were looking at Marny reflectively. "I believe you do, Marny, and there aren't many girls to whom one can say that nowadays. Love has become a careless game to them, and it's inclined to make a man a little afraid."

His remark vaguely troubled her, for it took her mind back to that scene she had interrupted between him and Ilena a couple of weeks before. She had been troubled by his manner at that time, she recalled. He had been angry . . . but he had also been hurt and rather bewildered. It was as though some doubt concerning Ilena had crept into his heart that evening and Marny couldn't help feeling that he referred to her when he spoke of girls treating love like a game.

She took an iced biscuit off the coffee-tray and nibbled it. Paul had spooned some cream into a saucer for Tiger and he was lapping it with greedy purrs and getting a great deal of it over his face and whiskers. As Paul laughed at him, some of the tension eased out of his face, and Marny thought he looked like a big boy with his hair in his eyes as usual and his teeth showing square and white. She liked him very much, and resentment stirred in her that Ilena might be making him unhappy.

After a while he began to talk about some of his patients, and the talk suddenly veered round to Ginger. Now the boy's X-rays had been taken and the region of damage fully explored, Paul said he wanted to operate as soon as possible. But there was a snag. Before he could perform the operation, Ginger's mother had to be found. She had walked out on him three years before, but that made no difference to the fact that her signature was needed on a consent form before Paul could help the child she hadn't wanted.

"Ironical, isn't it?" Paul offered Marny a cigarette and lit it for her. Then he lit his own. "She's half to blame for the way the boy is, yet I can't do a darn thing towards really helping him until she gives her official okay. When she left Farning she went up north to live with another man. Since then she appears to have broken with him and gradually drifted downhill. There isn't much doubt about how she's living now, and the police should get a line on her fairly soon. The trouble is, these women will use half a dozen different names."

"Will you really be able to make Ginger well and strong again?" Marny regarded him eagerly.

"I'm going to have a darn good try, honey." He smiled at her eagerness. "Thanks to you his nerves are in a much better state than they were, and he eats well. There is one thing, though, I've noticed that you seem to spend most of your off-duty time with him. You should get away from the Clinic now and again."

"I like being with Ginger," she said at once. "I feel so sorry for him. Do you know, Mr. Stillman, he's never been to the seaside." Her eyes met Paul's, dark and hurt for the boy. "He's never paddled in the sea, or collected shells, or made sand pies. I used to love doing all those things when I was a child, and my father would sit me high on his shoulders and walk right out into the water with me, until I wasn't a bit afraid of it and I just swam as naturally as a fish." She hugged her knees and her eyes had grown soft and reflective. "I adored my father. He had a wonderful, vital smile and a heart as big as a house. He was very tall, like you, Mr. Stillman, and my mother used to look so tiny beside him. He could lift her into the air as easily as he could lift me."

"It's a grand thing to have had a happy childhood," Paul agreed. "My folks were farmers. They worked awful hard and didn't always reap the rewards they deserved for all their labour, but laughter wasn't ever rationed in our old kitchen in the lean times. Pop died when I was sixteen and Drew, my brother, took Ma and me away from the farm. He'd graduated from college the year before and turned ice-hockey professional. He put me through medical school. I owe Drew a lot."

"Is that how he hurt his back, playing ice-hockey?" Marny asked. "Scotty told me that you developed an interest in osteopathy through some spinal trouble your brother had."

"That's right. Drew received a bad kick in the back during a match and shortly afterwards he began to bend over like an old

77

man. He couldn't seem to straighten up at all. He had to give up the game and he was in and out of different hospitals for several months, having tests and sunray treatments. None of them helped him, and finally his wife, Stella, persuaded him to go and see an osteopath she'd heard about." Paul smiled down into Marny's absorbed face. "The body's a funny thing, Marny. One little cog out of gear, especially in the spinal region, and it can go completely to pieces.

"Well, that osteopath took Drew in hand, and I was mighty impressed by the way he had him upright and fit in less than three months, whereas ordinary medical treatment had failed to help him. The hospitals had used drugs and sunray lamps, but that osteopath just used his hands, like a gardener coaxing a patch of ground that had once yielded well and then gone suddenly arid. Drew even went back to ice-hockey for a while, but unfortunately that kick had slowed him up as far as the game was concerned, so he quit altogether and went into the restaurant business. He's done pretty well for himself, too. My mother died soon after Drew retired from professional ice-hockey and I came over here to study osteopathy."

Paul glanced down at his hands and Marny watched him flex his slender fingers. "Would it sound like a cliché, Marny, if I said I loved my work?" he asked.

"I know you love it," she replied warmly. "That's one of the reasons I'm so glad I'm of use here."

"All the same," his eyes moved over her face, which showed signs this morning of the restless night she'd had, "I'm not having you overworking and not taking any relaxation away from the Clinic. We've all got to unwind now and again. Look, you were saying just now that Ginger's never been to the seaside. Let's remedy that, Marny." His eyes grew eager. "Let's take him to see the sand and the sea. We could go on Saturday. Alec

Gordon won't mind looking after things for me here at the Clinic, and Ilena, as you know, is in Paris. We've nothing to stop us and the weather's just right for a day by the sea."

A day by the sea, with Ginger and Paul! Marny didn't, at this time, question the extent of her delight in the idea, but she at once suggested that they go to Knighton Sands. "There's a lovely cove there," she told Paul, hugging Tiger as he leapt into her lap, "and the sands are almost silver. I was taken there once or twice as a child and I loved it. It's rather a nice run as well. We pass the New Forest, and Ginger will be able to see the ponies and deer."

"You're just as eager to see the ponies and deer yourself, aren't you?" Paul laughed, watching her as she rubbed Tiger under the chin. The cat purred with pleasure, full of cream and wholeheartedly enjoying the novelty of being held by someone who felt nice and soft and who didn't puff cigar smoke over his coat every now and again.

It was a bit of a novelty for Paul as well, to see someone like Marny in his sitting-room, her slender legs tucked under her in an engagingly unsophisticated way, and her youthful arms, just touched with down as the sun slanted on them, cradled about Tiger's big, furry body. Her dark hair, he noticed, drained her skin to a clear, delicate whiteness as it fell against her neck.

"There's a child in all of us, I think," she said. She looked at him and a smile darted across her face. "I've seen you playing snakes and ladders with Ginger!"

"I plead guilty to reading his comics occasionally as well," Paul laughed, and they unanimously agreed on Knighton Sands for their outing. He said he'd get Mrs. Piper, his housekeeper, to pack a picnic lunch for them and suggested that Marny go shopping the following day for a pair of swimming trunks for Ginger. Also she might get him a coloured bucket and a spade.

"And now we'd better get back to work," he got to his feet and dotted the end of his cigarette, "or the staff will be without their wages tomorrow."

Marny's hip turned plum-black and Paul refused to let her work the following day. He assured her there was no damage to her hip-bone, but he said it wouldn't hurt her to have a morning's rest in bed. She obediently rested, but she got up for lunch and afterwards went out shopping for herself and some of the nurses. When she arrived back at the Clinic she decided to have her tea under the big Lebanon cedar that stood in the grounds. She was just carrying her tray out of the bungalow when she saw Errol Dennis strolling across from the Clinic. She waited for him.

"You can join me, if you like to get yourself a cup and saucer," she said.

He hurried into the bungalow after the cup and saucer, for he definitely liked the idea of joining her. He had, in fact, come to see how she was.

"It turned me pretty sick when I felt the car hit you." His tawny eyes flashed over her as he stood with his back to the cedar stirring his tea. "You are all right?"

"I'm bruised, but I'll live. Will you have a biscuit?" She smiled and held out a plate and he accepted a chocolate wafer. "Anyway, the accident wasn't entirely your fault."

"Stillman seemed to think it was. He ticked me off." Errol crunched his biscuit, but he didn't look too upset by the fact that he had been 'ticked off', and as Marny watched him, she wondered at his complete self-containment. It was true he had looked shaken up when his car had knocked her down the other day, but she felt that he took very little to heart.

It was a sultry day, and this was rather worrying Marny. She didn't want the weather to break up and spoil the outing which she and Paul had planned for the following day. Ginger had been told, and she couldn't bear to think of his disappointment if the outing had to be called off.

"We're in for a bit of a storm, from the look of that sky," Errol remarked. The sun lay in red, shredded bars across the sky and the bluish-green leaves of the cedar kept shifting and rattling, as though a hand shook them. Errol drank his tea, a shine of perspiration on his upper lip. Marny had twisted her hair into a loose pony-tail in an attempt to keep cool, but each moment the air seemed to grow smokily hotter.

"Stillman must have nerves of iron," Errol said. "I'm damned if I could face his job today."

Every other Friday Paul went to a little hospital at Stepney, where most of the patients were permanent cripples. There wasn't much hope of effecting cures for many of them, but osteopathic manipulation and massage did bring some of them a certain amount of relief, and Paul worked in conjunction with a fellow osteopath, Martin Stein.

"You don't like Mr. Stillman very much, do you, Errol?" Marny said.

He shrugged his shoulders and held his lighter to Marny's cigarette. "Let's say a chemical animosity operates between us. We both feel it and can't control it. Law of the jungle, perhaps. I admire his abilities and he admires mine, and as far as work goes we're compatible. But, faith, we're not compatible where anything else is concerned." Smoke drifted from Errol's lips and his mobile eyebrows expressed a wry mingling of amusement and impatience. "That guy sits in judgment on my tendency to appreciate the opposite sex, but he's been no saint in his time." Errol flicked ash sharply. "Reformed rakes make damned conventional husbands. I hope the glamorous Ilena is prepared to accept this."

81

"I don't think Mr. Stillman's ever been a rake," Marny quickly protested. "I admit that he's attractive to women –"

"Do you find him attractive?" Errol's eyes had gone narrow and cat-like as they searched her face. "When you're alone with him in that office of his, does he ever make passes at you?"

"No, he doesn't!" The extent of Marny's indignation even surprised herself. She shook with it as she got up out of her garden chair and went to stand beyond the shade which the big tree threw. It was as though she had to withdraw from proximity with Errol for a moment or two. "Mr. Stillman's an engaged man," she said stiffly, "and Ilena is the most beautiful creature I've ever seen."

" 'Thy wife shall be as a fruitful vine by the side of thine house,' " Errol murmured, with a cynical smile. "Wicked as I am, I know my Bible, you see, Marny."

Marny swung to face him and her green eyes grew rather frightened as they dwelt on his lean, sardonic face. "What has that quotation to do with Ilena?" she demanded.

"Sure now, I think you know, though you probably don't want to know – for our dear Paul Stillman's sake. She'll be deadly nightshade beside a man's house, not a fruitful vine."

Marny stared at Errol. She had thought that nothing could disturb Errol's composure, but now she saw that he had gone queerly white about the lips. Was it the heat that had whitened his lips, or some emotion, connected with Ilena, which he shouldn't be feeling?

Before she could stop herself she said to him: "Do you know Ilena so well?"

His glance dwelt on the bruised, fiery sky. "Let's say I use my eyes." He laughed and began to talk about the Chardmore Ball, to which Alec Gordon *might* agree to come as an escort for Julie Brelson. At the moment, however, he was fighting his widowed mother's determination that he shouldn't. Alec, poor blighter, Errol said, was too darn soft where his mother was concerned.

Marny listened inattentively to Errol, unable to dismiss his strange references to Ilena. What could he know about her? What could he know about the girl Paul loved that made him refer to her as deadly nightshade? Deadly nightshade was a poisonous plant. As Marny tried to read his face, the sky darkened overhead and there was a rumble of approaching thunder. Rain pattered on the leaves of the cedar, and Errol suddenly took Marny's cigarette from her fingers and dropped it to the grass with his own. As his shoes flattened the stubs, he drew her against his thin blue shirt, tightening his hands on her arms as she tried to pull free of him.

"Will you come out with me tomorrow evening?" he asked.

"I – I'm sorry, Errol, but Mr. Stillman is taking Ginger to the seaside tomorrow, and I'm going with them."

"I see." Errol's good-looking face was cynical. She flushed, for she knew exactly what he was thinking – that Paul was taking advantage of Ilena's visit to Paris to have a flirtation with her.

She glanced away from his eyes. "I think I'll go in now," she said. "It's starting to rain."

"Damn you!" he growled, and with surprisingly strong arms he held her immobile against him as he possessed her startled mouth in a kiss that left it stinging long after he strode towards the white Clinic building.

To Marny's intense relief Saturday morning dawned bright and sunny. It was as though the storm the day before had invigorated the earth, for everything looked sparkling and refreshed.

Mrs. Piper had packed a large picnic hamper, and while

Paul stowed it away in the back of the car, along with Ginger's bucket and spade and a big bag of apples for the New Forest ponies, Marny and the boy settled themselves in the front seat. Ginger was grinning all over his face and wearing a small facsimile of Paul's gay plaid shirt, (a purchase Marny had been unable to resist) tucked into a small pair of dungarees. Marny was also at ease in toreador pants and a sleeveless blouse, and as the car swept away from the Clinic, the trio might have been a small family party setting out for a day of carefree relaxation.

Mrs. Piper waved them off with a thoughtful smile. She had been with Paul since he had first opened the Clinic and she took his welfare very much to heart. He wanted Miss Justine, who was, of course, very beautiful, but one look at him with Miss Marny and the little crippled boy was enough to show how he felt about young things. He would want a family, but Mrs. Piper couldn't help wondering if he had yet consulted his fiancée on this point.

The black Bentley bowled along through the early morning city streets, where pigeons flirted on rooftops, their plumage looking metallic in the sunshine, and gay boxes of flowers decorated the windowsills of the tall office buildings. Paul shot a smile at Marny.

"Thank heaven yesterday's storm didn't break up the weather," he remarked.

"Yes, thank heaven," Ginger murmured, carefully stripping the wrapping off a bar of milk chocolate. Marny and Paul burst out laughing and their eyes met for a moment above his young head. A soft wind through the car windows was blowing Marny's hair into a lovely disorder above her laughing green eyes and she looked like an embodiment of summer itself – warm, apricot-tinted, welcoming the touch of the sun.

"How very pretty you look, Marny," Paul said. "Like a gay

holiday poster."

The compliment did not confuse her, for she knew instinctively that Paul was not flirting with her. She smiled back at him, then accepted a rather sticky piece of chocolate from Ginger, who evidently considered it much more effective to feed a pretty girl with sweets rather than speeches.

His long-lashed eyes were bright with happiness as he sat between the two people who had almost blotted out his bad memories and shown him that he too was lovable, despite his crooked shoulder.

Ginger had unfortunately learned at the orphanage that there were people who distinguished between robust children and those with a physical disability. He had noticed that it was always the robust children who found new parents. Then they went to live in a nice house where there was a garden and very often a brother or a sister to play with, sometimes a dog as well. Getting adopted seemed far out of Ginger's reach, but in his heart, very, very secretly, he had adopted Marny and Mr. Stillman.

He hugged his secret to himself. They would be ever so surprised if they knew, he thought, and he glanced at Paul, then at Marny, in a proprietorial fashion. They were his two people, and he put his red head against Marny, who tickled his ribs and reduced him to a fit of the giggles.

They spent half an hour in the New Forest feeding the shaggy ponies from the windows of the car, and when they reached Knighton Sands, the sea was like silver lamé, laced with creamy foam as it ran in against this lovely, wild beach that had never attained to popularity with the masses, to whom a day at the seaside meant cockle stalls, ice-cream parlours and noisy fun-arcades. Here and there a solitary family party lay stretched on the silvery sand, mopping up the sunshine and happily dispensing with the noise and riot of the more popular beaches farther along the coast. Swallows dipped their wings as they flew low over the glittering water and the white and pearl-grey herring gulls wailed above the cliffs, where sea-beat and tangled ferns hung curtain-like over the cave openings in the cliff face.

Marny whipped off her shoes and ran barefoot across the soft sand. Ginger did the same and charged after her. They went right down to the water's edge, and Paul could hear their young laughter floating back to him. When they eventually returned, carrying some rather bedraggled sea convolvulus, he had the picnic hamper open and was obligingly spreading lunch. They tucked into chicken, salad and hard-boiled eggs, and afterwards Marny dozed for a while on the hot, fine sand. The silky murmuring of the sea mingled with the wailing of the gulls, and Ginger's light voice mingled with the deep, slightly grating timbre of Paul's. Marny smiled against her arm when Ginger said, softly and mischievously: "Marny's gone to sleep, Uncle Paul, and I'm gonna bury her in the sand."

A bucket of warm sand rained over her legs. It tickled, and she had to suppress a giggle. More sand, and Paul said lazily: "You'll cop it, young feller, when Marny wakes up and finds herself covered in sand."

"Oh, she won't mind." Ginger sounded very sure as he emptied his bucket over her again. "Marny's not a cry-baby like other girls. She's an extra special girl. She's seen otters, Uncle Paul, and she knows how to sail a boat. I bet there ain't – aren't many girls who could do that."

"I bet there aren't, old chap," Paul agreed, and he smiled as he sat watching Ginger busily burying Marny in the sand. Her influence over the boy was even noticeable in his speech, Paul reflected, and as he smoked his cigar he thought of her that very first day at the railway station. He had been startled by her youth, he remembered, and very doubtful that she'd fit in at the Clinic. She had more than fitted in. She had become almost indispensable to him, and he couldn't imagine not having her to talk to about the various difficulties that cropped up at the Clinic. She never intruded her opinion, but for someone so young she had an amazing capacity for winning people's confidence. She had helped him lately with a couple of really nervous patients. There was Mrs. Grant, a victim of deafness induced by a mastoid infection. She had come to him a couple of weeks ago, but the idea of undergoing finger surgery had frightened her. He had enlisted Marny's aid in talking to the woman and winning her round to the idea. She had now undergone the operation and was beginning to hear again after nine years of almost total deafness.

The sand was beginning to pile up on Marny and she heard Paul say: "I should make that do, Ginger. Marny's only a little thing, remember, and she's got a bruised hip."

"All right." Ginger obligingly curtailed his burying operations. "I think I'll go and play with that dog over there," he decided, and he marched off with his sandy bucket on his head, leaving Paul to dig Marny out of the sand.

"Ups-a-daisy!" He pulled her to her feet and brushed her down. "I think we've got time for a swim before the tide comes in. You didn't forget your suits, did you?"

"No fear! We'll change in that cave over there. What about you?"

"I've got my trunks on under my slacks."

"We shan't be long." She collected the bathing suits and went running across to the cave where Ginger was playing. He was raking about among the rocks that peppered this part of the beach, hunting for shiny stones. A very damp mongrel dog was helping him. Marny took the dog to belong to someone on the beach.

"His name's Blackie," Ginger informed her, giving the dog a pat on the head. "You're a lovely old boy, aren't you, Blackie?"

The dog barked a sound agreement with this sentiment, and Marny smiled. "We're going to have a swim, Ginger," she said. "Come and put your trunks on."

"Swimming?" He glanced up. "Me?"

"Yes, you!" She laughingly swung him to his feet and took the bucket off his head. "Uncle Paul will carry you on his shoulders. You won't be afraid, will you?"

"Nope!" He followed her into the cave, where she quickly. stripped off his clothes and put him into the green trunks she had bought him the day before.

"Can Blackie come swimmin' with us?" he asked, holding on to her shoulder as she pulled the trunks up over his thin young flanks.

"I don't see why not," she smiled. "From the look of him he's already been in the water, so his master can't mind. There, don't you look nice? Now you can join Uncle Paul while I put my suit on."

But suddenly the boy hesitated, then he wrapped his arms round her waist and pressed his face against her. "Will the people look at my shoulder?" he whispered.

"Of course not, darling." Marny hugged him gently. "Do you want to wait for me?"

"Yes, I'll wait for you." He went and sat in the cave entrance with the black mongrel, and Marny watched his distorted little back as she stripped and put on her white suit. Love for the child was an ache in her. How could anyone have hurt him so terribly, least of all his own father! He was an inoffensive child, and his refusal to look at her while she undressed revealed him

88

to be touchingly gallant. She pulled on her green rubber cap, and hand in hand she and Ginger walked down the beach to where Paul was skimming stones across the surface of the water. The black mongrel trotted along beside them.

"Uncle Paul!" Ginger called out.

Paul swung round from the water's edge. He looked hard and long-limbed in his trunks, the muscles running smoothly under his skin as he lifted Ginger to his shoulder. "I've room for another small one," he grinned down at Marny.

His arm was curving towards her when she fled nimbly past him into the water. "No ... no!" Her laughter was touched with panic.

The carefree, sunny hours sped away, and on the way home Ginger slept soundly, wrapped in a rug on the back seat of the car, while Marny dozed with her red-gold head just touching Paul's shoulder.

The smell of the sea was still on his skin, and Marny breathed him with a kind of dreamy pleasure. He was so very nice, she thought, and now she couldn't understand why something about him on the beach had sent her flying from his side in such a panic.

CHAPTER V

THE following afternoon Marny decided to go to Ilena's flat to collect the dragonfly costume which Nadia was lending her. She went over to the Clinic about two o'clock to ask Nadia for the door-key, then took a bus ride to Routledge Court in Knightsbridge, where Ilena lived.

She had no trouble finding Routledge Court, a smart, russet-brick building with a tiny mews at the side of it. Marny crossed the mews, and she at once noticed a low-slung, scarlet racing car parked in the kerb. The racer immediately put her in mind of Errol Dennis's, and her step faltered while she took in the dove-grey upholstery and tried to recall the registration number of Errol's car. Of course, this one didn't necessarily have to belong to him, but there was a remote possibility that he had forgotten Ilena was in Paris until tomorrow and he was calling on her.

Then Marny frowned.

Paul didn't like Errol. She couldn't see him remotely tolerating the thought of any social intercourse between his fiancé and any man whom he considered a philanderer. It had annoyed him, Marny reflected, that the good-looking Irishman had shown signs of wanting to start up a friendship with her.

Marny abruptly decided that plenty of people probably owned racy scarlet cars in a smart area like Knightsbridge, and on this reflection she walked into Routledge Court.

Nadia had said the flat was on the fifth floor, and Marny entered the lift and pressed the appropriate button. The lift travelled silently upwards, then the door slid open and she stepped out on to a landing whose quietness seemed intensified by the warm sunshine and the twittering of birds coming in through an open window.

Marny inserted the little Yale key in the lock of number nineteen and quietly opened the door on a square, carpeted hall-way. She had no trouble finding the cupboard in which Nadia's costume trunk was stored, and she drew it out, unlocked it and knelt to examine its contents. The costumes were fragile, gossamer-like, but some of Marny's enchantment in them was dimmed when she remembered that never again would Nadia spin across a stage in one of them. . . .

Then Marny glanced up sharply from the trunk. She turned her head and stared at the closed door of what she took to be the lounge of the flat. She was certain she had just heard the mutter of voices beyond that door, and a white, frilled ballet dress fell from her hands, back into the trunk, as she scrambled to her feet and faced round just as the door opened. She saw the shimmer of a kingfisher blue wrap, the bare whiteness of long, slender legs underneath it, then she and Ilena Justine were staring into one another's startled eyes.

Marny was struck speechless with embarrassment . . . and another emotion that felt awfully like fear. Fear snaked its way through her, and she flinched when Ilena sharply said: "What are *you* doing here?" She gestured with a Gallic passion and her fingernails glinted as though dipped in blood. "How dare you come slinking into my flat in this manner!"

"I . . ." Marny backed away from the angry passion of Ilena's face and voice, "I came to collect a costume Nadia is lending me. I had no idea you'd be here, Miss Justine. If I had known I should have rung the doorbell and not used Nadia's key. I — I'm terribly sorry I frightened you."

"Nadia has no right to give her door-key to all and sundry,"

Ilena returned bitingly, and one of her elegant hands caught agitatedly at the front of her wrap, as though she suddenly realized her *déshabille*. "I was resting on my bed after a bath, and I at once thought of burglars, hearing someone out here in the hallway."

"I'm sorry," Marny said again, and she hardly knew that she was staring at the strange wildness of Ilena's eyes until the other girl snapped at her:

"Why do you look at me like that? What is the matter?"

"Mr. Stillman said you were returning from Paris tomorrow—"

"I changed my mind." Ilena's accented voice had grown rather discordant. "Is it so strange that I should change my mind?"

"No, of course not."

"There was some trouble in Paris—I wanted to get away." Ilena's petrol-blue eyes swept over the trunk beside Marny, then her velvet wrap opened, showing her shapely legs as she stepped across the hallway and stood gazing down into Nadia's trunk. "Which costume is my cousin lending you?" she asked. "Is it for the Chardmore Ball?"

Marny nodded, relieved that Ilena had decided to forget her anger. She explained that Nadia was lending her the dragonfly costume. "We both wanted to find out whether it needed any alterations before the twenty-fourth, and I suppose I wanted to see how I looked in it," Marny added with a smile.

"The dragonfly costume, eh?" Ilena's glance travelled over Marny. During working hours at the Clinic the girl invariably wore blouses and skirts and occasionally a light cotton dress, but today she wore a leaf-green shantung dress with a matching bandeau about her hair. Green sandals complemented her dress, and she looked so pretty and cool that Ilena's eyes went narrow and she wasn't too pleased by the realization that Paul's secretary could look like this when she wanted to.

Ilena began to pull costumes out of Nadia's trunk with long-nailed, careless hands. "So you are going to the *fête champêtre* as a dragonfly – a little childish, but appropriate enough." Ilena smiled thinly. "Have you found yourself an escort yet"

"I'm going with Errol Dennis," Marny replied.

"With whom?"

"Mr. Dennis, who works at the Clinic." At that moment Marny came upon the costume she was looking for, and she was so busy admiring it that she didn't notice for a moment that Ilena had returned to the lounge. The French girl was standing by an informal table of bird's eye maple, lighting a cigarette, when Marny joined her.

"This is a delightful costume, isn't it, Miss Justine?" she enthused. "It has exactly the metallic gleam of a dragonfly, and there's even a suggestion of sulphur in this blue-green colour."

Ilena puffed smoke towards wine-red taffeta curtains, through which the sun slanted in a bright beam, diffusing its gold over the ivory walls of the room and making the big diamond on Ilena's hand flame with blue-white fire.

"Errol Dennis is your beau?" Ilena asked.

"Of course not!" Marny laughed at the idea.

"But you are going to the Chardmore Ball with him, so you must find him an agreeable companion," Ilena insisted.

"He can be quite nice," Marny agreed, "but he's a shocking flirt." She stood fondling the glittering wings of the costume in her hands, and talking of Errol reminded her of that scarlet car parked in the mews beside this block of flats. For some reason her heart suddenly fluttered like a small wild bird. Her glance ran round the smart lounge, taking in its expensive fittings, its air of luxury and self-indulgence.

93

"Mr. Dennis flirts with you, *petite*?" Ilena's petrol-blue eyes dwelt narrowly on the carnation pink that stole into Marny's cheeks. "Ah, I see that he does! Well, he is exceedingly handsome, so I am sure you must find his attentions most flattering!"

Marny only knew that she found this conversation rather distasteful. She couldn't like Ilena as she liked Nadia, for this girl was without her cousin's fundamental warmth of heart. She was primitive as a tigress, with the same jungle beauty, the same desire to draw blood and dip her cruel, dainty paws in it.

A man's woman, perhaps, Marny thought, but she was not likeable.

"Have you decided on a costume for the Ball yet, Miss Justine?" Marny enquired.

"I am going as a water-sylph. My costume is still at the makers, otherwise I would show it to you." Ilena was now wandering restlessly about the lounge, and Marny caught the glimpse of black lace lingerie under her shimmering wrap. "Paul, you know, is going as a lumberjack. I should have preferred him to wear a costume that would have complemented mine, which is silver, but he can be so awkward at times."

Marny repressed a quick smile. She didn't doubt for a moment that Paul had turned awkward about wearing a showy costume to the Ball, for he always seemed at his happiest in casual tweeds or a plaid shirt worn Yankee style outside his slacks.

Ilena, mad on clothes, seemed to be reflecting on Paul's lack of interest in them, for she stabbed her cigarette angrily hard into an ashtray. "Now, *petite*, I shall not detain you any longer," she said. "I am feeling rather tired."

"I expect it's been a busy week for you," Marny agreed.

"Yes. Line Cabot is designing my wedding dress, and she has rather frayed my nerves, she insists on so many fittings."

94

Ilena yawned delicately and her heavy-lidded glance strayed to a door at the far end of the lounge. It stood a little ajar, and Marny saw the rich white carpet and crystal jars glinting on a dressing-table.

"Would you mind re-packing Nadia's costumes?" Ilena asked.

"Of course not, Miss Justine." Marny returned to the hall-way, where she laid the fragile costumes back in their wrap-ping paper and the mothballs that no longer emitted any odour after two years. She locked the trunk and slid it back into the hall cupboard. Then she carefully folded the dragonfly costume and put it into the dress-bag she had brought with her.

"I'm going now, Miss Justine," she called out.

Ilena at once came to the doorway of the lounge. "*Petite,*" she spoke rather tensely, "I do not wish Nadia to know there was trouble in Paris yesterday, she would be unduly alarmed. It is trouble that involved René Blanchard, therefore be dis-creet. Do not mention that I am home today – to anyone."

Marny gazed back at her employer's fiancée with troubled eyes, too concerned for Nadia to really notice the emphasis which Ilena had put upon those last two words. "May I know what happened?" Marny asked. "I promise I shan't say any-thing to Nadia."

"There was a bombing raid outside the Santé prison yes-terday morning. René was being taken back there after giving evidence in court, and it is thought that a group of students are attempting to take his life. They did not succeed yesterday, but a guard was badly hurt."

"But isn't he a student leader himself?" Marny looked rather bewildered.

Ilena shrugged her shoulder. "French politics are very invol-ved. René was sympathetic towards the students and this par-

95

ticular group think he has let them down. René now stands between two fires, and though he has been a fool, one must have a little compassion for him." Ilena gestured dramatically. "That business yesterday, it was most upsetting. I – I could not stay in Paris, but if Nadia knew I had returned so hurriedly she would insist that I tell her why. So, please, it might be advisable if you forget you have seen me here today."

Ilena's smile was suddenly coaxing and charming. She even held out a hand towards Marny, who didn't take it as she said: "Very well, Miss Justine. Goodbye!"

Marny walked to the bus stop, where she stood slim and quiet in her leaf-green dress, the bandeau about her hair fluttering in a fresh, summery breeze.

She was intensely glad to be out of Ilena's flat ... a sort of scented cage where she had left hemmed in by the elegant luxury and untamed beauty of the tall French girl, a shimmering wrap tied carelessly about her exquisite body, revealing far more than it covered. Marny tried to control the feeling of antagonism that swept through her, while she determinedly shut her mind against the knowledge that there *had* been a mutter of voices in the lounge, before Ilena had opened the door.

Marny's bus swept into the kerb. Impulsively she let it go and took another as far as Hyde Park. There she walked alone in the park for about an hour, until she remembered that she was having tea with Ginger, who would be disappointed if she failed to turn up.

A couple of weeks later the police got a line on Ginger's mother, and Paul went to see her that same afternoon, at an address in the East End of London.

She turned out to be a blowsy, carroty creature, with the hard expression of her calling and a decayed kind of beauty. Her

96

eyes, brown and long-lashed like her son's, moved over Paul with professional speculation when she answered her landlady's bellowing call up the stairs of this tenement house in which she had a back room. He was a bit classy, compared to the sort that usually knocked here, but nothing very much could surprise Nell Farning any more.

"Comin' up?" She jerked a hand towards the stairs, and a smell of rancid cooking fat and cheap scent clutched at Paul's throat as he followed the woman up to her room. Her down-at-heel slippers showed the callouses on her feet, and Paul saw varicose veins marring legs that still belonged to a woman under thirty.

"Come along in, love." She shut the door on them, and Paul's cold grey glance swept round the room, taking in the grimy net curtains at the one window, the chipped wash-stand and pile of cheap American magazines on a table beside the bed. A black nylon suspender-belt hung over the brass rail of the bed and some other bits and pieces of clothing spilled out of a cupboard beside the fireplace.

Nell Farning stared at her caller.

She knew men and the world too well, and instinct suddenly told her that this man wasn't calling on the likes of her for the usual purpose. She flicked a nylon stocking off the floor and thrust it under the eiderdown of her bed. "Are you a copper?" she wanted to know.

His mouth twitched slightly and he shook his head. "I've come to talk to you about your son, Mrs. Farning."

"Oh, yeah?" A smaller flicker of surprise did show in her brown eyes this time. She took a packet of Woodbines off the mantelpiece and slowly shook one into her hand. "Got a light, love?"

He spun the wheel of his lighter and she leant towards the

flame, her dressing-gown falling open at the neck to reveal the delicate, blue-veined skin that invariably accompanies most shades of red hair. Paul felt a flicker of pity for the creature. An evanescent beauty had been hers, but she had fallen into the clutches of a brute and all illusion had been torn out of her.

"So you've come about Ginger, 'ave you?" she said. "Well, what about him? You some sort of welfare bloke who wants me to 'elp support him?" She laughed coarsely. "I can barely support myself at times. To make money these days you've got to be a stripper – can you see me stripping with these legs?" She held back a fold of her dressing-gown and showed him the hard, knotted veins of her thighs. "Occupational hazard." She laughed again, then choked on a mouthful of cigarette smoke. "I think the kid better grow up quick, so he can 'elp support his poor old mother."

"I'm an osteopath, Mrs. Farning," Paul informed her coldly, "and your son is a patient at my Clinic. You are aware, I suppose, that your husband injured the boy very badly about eighteen months ago? His right shoulder-blade was broken, and because he didn't receive proper medical attention until some days afterwards the bone failed to mend correctly. I'm going to have a try at putting that damage right. This entails an operation, and I must have your signature on this consent form." Paul opened his pocket-book and withdrew the form. "I take it you're agreeable to the operation, Mrs. Farning?"

"Why not? The kid won't get much of a job later on if he isn't put right." She took the form and without troubling to read it asked for a pen.

Paul handed her his fountain pen, and his eyes were suddenly frosty with temper, while all pity for her sputtered out of him. That youngster meant nothing to this creature, beyond the chance that later on he might help to support her, when her looks had completely deserted her and she was no longer able to attract men.

She handed the form back to him, with her signature sprawled carelessly across the bottom. Helen Maud Farning.

Paul returned the form to his pocket-book, then he strode to the door and opened it. "Don't you want to see Ginger?" he coldly asked. "You must have some feeling for him."

"Really?" She had followed him to the door, and now she lolled against the wall, cigarette smoke drifting from her lips and her shabby dressing-gown revealing the slackening lines of her figure. Her eyes travelled over Paul, taking deliberate note of his good grooming, his tailored suit and speckless shoes. "Your sort hasn't got a clue, mister," she said. "You get born in some dockside slum next time round. Get born a fairly good-looking girl and find yerself dragged into the yard of a warehouse one dark night by a toughie like Mike Farning. See if you're all starry-eyed about the result of such a romantic union. My dad made Mike marry me, but I never blessed him for interfering. I could 'ave given the kid to the Salvation Army. They'd 'ave got him adopted before Mike Farning got the chance to lay his brutal hands on him. Anyway," she shrugged and glanced at the cigarette in her hand, "what good would it do, me comin' to see him? There ain't much I can do for him. I don't suppose he even remembers me."

"He remembers enough, Mrs. Farning," Paul retorted, rather cuttingly. "He remembers things a child shouldn't have to remember, so I guess it wouldn't be a wise move for you to come and see him."

She bit her lip at that, then resorted to insolence when Paul had stepped out on to the musty landing of the house. "Don't forget where I live, good-looking. Come back another time, when you haven't got business on your mind," she invited.

His frosty glance swept her from head to foot, then he was running down the stairs to the street.

Driving back to the Clinic, Paul thought of the happy day which he and Marny had spent with Ginger at Knighton Sands. Marny was teaching the boy so many things. Teaching him to lose the fears which had haunted him from a baby, showing him the love he had never had from his mother.

Mother!

The word didn't apply to Nell Farning, and Paul angrily rejected the thought that she might take Ginger back to her environment one day. Back to the squalor of a frowsy room such as the one she lived in at the moment, its walls and ceiling bruised by damp patches, its one window looking out on a bedraggled back yard.

Marny was busily typing when Paul walked into the office, but she stopped when she heard his step and swivelled round in her chair. His expression was rather grim, and she at once jumped to the conclusion that he had failed to acquire Mrs. Farning's consent to Ginger's operation.

"Didn't she sign the consent form, Mr. Stillman?" Marny rose to her feet and hurried across the room to him. She stood facing him, and after a moment he took her by the shoulders.

"Yes, she signed it, without even bothering to read it," he said wryly.

Marny relaxed. "Then everything's all right! You said you could go ahead with the operation once you'd got the mother's consent."

Paul's fingers felt the thin eagerness of Marny's bones, the passionate desire in her that he make Ginger well and strong again. This desire should have been in Nell Farning, but none of this had been in the woman who had borne Ginger. "It's all right, Marny," he spoke gently, "Ginger shall get his chance

100

to be like other boys. You want it very badly, don't you?"

She nodded, and her body was as fluently aware of Paul's sympathy as he was of hers. It was as though for one strange moment they merged into a single unity, swept by the desire that this child be made happy. An idea had begun to formulate at the back of Paul's mind during the drive back here to the Clinic, and in this moment it took definite shape. But first he said to Marny: "Buzz the kitchen and have them make some coffee, honey. I've a devil of a thirst."

Coffee was brought in, and Paul paced about the office with his cup in his hand, describing in detail his visit to Nell Farning and her reception of his wish to operate on her son and try to remedy the damage caused by her husband.

"That blowsy slut didn't care a cotton-picking damn about how sick he'd be for a while, so long as he gets put right for later on, when he can work and pay for her cigarettes and clothes." Paul paused by the glass doors, where he stood tall and brooding for several long moments, then Marny heard him take one of those deep, decisive breaths he usually took when he was making a definite diagnosis about a patient.

"There's only one way I know of to ensure a decent future for that boy, and that's for me to adopt him." Paul slowly turned to look at Marny. "I've grown fond of him, too."

Marny carefully lowered her coffee cup into her saucer, for her hands were suddenly unsteady. "You're — going to adopt Ginger?" she breathed.

Paul inclined his dark head. "I shall have to discuss the matter with Ilena, of course, but I shouldn't think she'd object. Ginger's a good kid." He strolled to his desk and stood smiling down at Marny. "D'you think the boy will like me for a father?" he asked.

"Yes, Mr. Stillman!" There wasn't a scrap of doubt in her,

101

for Paul was too like her own father for a child not to adore him. Gladness swept through her, warming her, like a caress.

Paul's eyes grew boyish. "I haven't had much practice with children, honey, but I take it you think I'll be able to win the boy's affection?"

"You have his affection already." Her voice was soft. "Didn't you know?"

"Well," a slightly diffident note crept into Paul's voice, "the affection of other people isn't a thing we like to be too sure about. It's a will-o'-the-wisp which we sometimes follow blindly across a wasteland of other emotions. I didn't want to make the mistake of taking Ginger's gratitude for affection."

"You won't be making a mistake, Mr. Stillman." Marny could have hugged Paul breathless for wanting to adopt Ginger, and her wish was transmitted to him by the way she caught at his hand and squeezed it. "When will you tell Ginger?" she asked.

"Maybe tomorrow." He smiled into Marny's green, glowing eyes. "I'm dining at Ilena's place tonight, so I shall definitely broach the subject."

"Do you – think she'll be agreeable?" Now Marny slipped her fingers free of Paul's, and he strolled to the big chair behind his desk. After he had lit a cigar, he sat with his feet comfortably propped on a corner of the desk.

"Ilena isn't exactly a predictable person," he admitted, "but I shan't ask her to behave like the boy's mother. Mrs. Piper will be living with us at Henley-on-Thames, where I'm buying a house, and she's a good-hearted, capable woman. I think the arrangement will work out."

He turned his cigar about in his fingers and regarded the sharp end of it. The aromatic smoke drifted towards Marny and her leaf-brown lashes fluttered down tremulously over her eyes, and she tried to thrust resentment of Ilena out of her thoughts. Ilena, who might have Ginger for always, but who wouldn't want to behave like his mother.

Oh, she was utterly beautiful, of course. Marny could understand a man wanting to possess that exquisite body, that matt-white skin, that almost Eastern allure, but what had Ilena to offer apart from it? Had she the pride in Paul she should have. Had she an overwhelming desire to serve one man all her life?

"I want to give the boy security and a good education, Marny," Paul went on. "He's got a quick little mind — have you noticed? He's imaginative, and sensitive to colour and form. There are possibilities in him which aren't going to be blasted to nothing by that — that creature I saw this afternoon." Paul's teeth clenched angrily on his cigar. "It amazes me that she and that brute Farning should have made such a child . . . in damned ugly circumstances, too."

"Perhaps he inherits traits from way back in either her family or the husband's," Marny suggested. "I mean, take Nadia and your fiancée. You can see they have Russian blood, though they're of French parentage."

"That's true," Paul agreed. He smiled to himself as he reflected on Ilena's exotic beauty and turbulent temper at times. The invading hordes of Ghengis Khan had carried Tartar blood into Russia long, long ago, and Ilena, in the twentieth century, bore unmistakable traces of that invasion — more so than Nadia.

Heredity was certainly a strange and wonderful thing, he thought. Like the whole of life, really. The wonder of breathing and moving. The miracle of touch and sight. The impulse to want and be wanted.

His grey eyes stole over the girl who sat beside his desk,

and there suddenly drifted into his mind a vague wonder what a child of hers would be like. A sprightly imp, no doubt, with the assured eyes of a child who knew itself wanted with every fibre of that slender body of Marny's, which had to the touch a warm, bird-like breakability.

He flicked cigar ash, and now his glance brooded on a framed photograph of Ilena that stood on his desk.

She wore a fur Cossack hat and a slightly enigmatic smile played at the corners of her small, provocative mouth. The photograph had been taken on the day of their engagement, and something she said that day returned to his mind in this moment. She had quoted a Spanish proverb: "He loves thee well who makes thee weep", then she had said: "I may make you want to weep at times, Paul, but never forget that I love you."

He touched the frame of the photograph with his slender fingers. Strange, lovely Ilena!

Then abruptly he swung his feet down off his desk. "I'd better get my letters signed," he said. "Afterwards you might be a good girl, Marny, and pop them round to the post."

"Certainly, Mr. Stillman." Marny handed his letters across the desk and for a moment their fingers brushed. He smiled at her, noticing that today her hair was swirled to the top of her head and secured with a green velvet ribbon that matched her eyes. She looked cute, he thought. He'd never keep her here at the Clinic indefinitely. Some man was bound to want her before very long.

CHAPTER VI

THOUGH Paul had made up his mind to talk to Ilena that evening about adopting Ginger, it turned out that he didn't get the chance.

When he arrived at Ilena's flat he found Monsieur Justine there with several of his Embassy associates. Paul thought they had just dropped in for a drink, and he was decidedly annoyed when he learned they had been invited to dinner. He had been looking forward to a quiet, intimate dinner with Ilena, but instead the evening was devoted to student unrest in France.

When Ilena went to her bedroom for a handkerchief, Paul left Monsieur Justine and his friends arguing with Gallic noisiness and followed his fiancée. He closed the bedroom door and crossed the room to her, then closed his hands on her waist.

"Why the party, Ilena, when we were going to have this evening to ourselves?" His annoyed grey eyes searched her face, and now he noticed that she was looking rather pale and tense. "You look as though you could have done with a quiet evening. Aren't you sleeping well?"

"Not too well." She rested her forehead against him. "Oh, *chéri*, I wish it were October."

"Do you?" His arms drew her close to him. "Well, we don't have to wait till then, my dear. A big smart wedding was your idea, but you know I'd settle for something quicker and quieter."

He felt her stir restlessly against him.

"Paul, you have got to understand. Nadia's father has been

like my own father all these years, and I am fond of him. But he is a sentimental man, a little old-fashioned, I suppose, and the things he wishes for Nadia he wishes for me, also. He has said that Maman would have been proud to see me in a lovely white gown, surrounded by friends on my wedding day. She and my own father ran away to marry, and theirs was never a happy marriage. She died when I was born –" Ilena's breath caught on a sigh, then she glanced up into Paul's face, her lashes like points of jet about her petrol-blue eyes, her mouth all pouting curves like a rather unhappy child's. "I – I try to do things to please people. I do try, Paul," she almost whimpered.

She was trembling a little in the golden-gorse silk that clung to the curvaceous stem of her, and Paul was touched to a quick concern as he held her. He cupped her chin in one hand, but when he would have searched her eyes, she threw her arms about his neck and drew his head down to her. "Kiss me," she breathed against his mouth.

Their lips touched. He felt the tensing of her body, then the passionate yielding, and they kissed almost desperately, as though they each had thoughts that needed to be blotted out in this moment. A tiny moan of pain broke from Ilena, for Paul unknowingly crushed her against his dinner-jacket, then at last he drew away from her.

"We'd better be getting back to your other guests." He smiled in a wry way and wiped her poppy-red lipstick from his mouth. "Why the devil did you invite them, Ilena? I think we'd have both enjoyed being alone tonight."

"Perhaps they will leave early." The smile she gave him was suddenly full of allure. "Now go and mix drinks for me, daarling. You have robbed me of most of my lipstick and I must repaint my mouth."

She sat down at her dressing-table and their eyes met for

a moment in the mirror. He grinned, raked the dark hair back from his eyes, then returned to the lounge.

Often in the next hour Ilena's glance was upon Paul's face, and he wasn't unaware that tonight she was queerly strung up, wanting to be alone with him and yet, he felt, a little afraid of him. Her uncle and his friends did leave early, and when Ilena returned to the lounge after bidding them goodnight, she found Paul sitting on the couch with his head at rest against the wine-red velvet. Ilena knelt on the couch beside him and watched his face. It was a strong, deceptively hard face, with shadow caught in the deep cleft in his chin.

She touched his cheek and his grey eyes shot wide open when she whispered: "Stay with me tonight, *chéri*. I don't care to be alone . . . I want you with me."

Her whispered words and her perfume mingled enticingly together, then her heavy eyelids lifted and Paul saw that her eyes shimmered with a kind of feverish insistence.

"No, Ilena," he spoke decisively. "You're strung up after your trip to Paris, and I'd be a brute to take advantage of the fact."

"*Mon dieu,* the contrariness of men!" She sprang off the couch and her body had a tigerish tenseness. "Am I not re-membering now that you are a man and not a pet dog on a lead?"

"Honey," he stood up and caught hold of her hands, which quivered like wild birds as he held them, "you're a little un-well, I think. Your pulse is racing and you obviously need a good night's sleep."

"Oh, you smug devil!" She wrenched her hands free of his, and suddenly she was swept by one of her turbulent rages. She stamped a foot frenziedly and there was no colour in her face but the petrol-blue shimmer of her eyes. "It would seem that the rumours are true," she cried out. "It would seem that you do find your little secretary attractive – and accommodating!"

Her hysterical outburst whitened his face and his light eyes glinted frostily as he stood above her. "What damned rumours are you talking about?" he demanded. "Who's been telling you lies about Marny and myself?"

"Nadia, of course! She has heard certain things, a-and you took the girl to the seaside. Having the crippled child with the two of you must have cramped your style, Paul."

For a moment he could hardly believe that he heard her correctly, then, impelled by a sudden blistering anger, his hands reached out and closed bruisingly on her shoulders. He shook her so hard that her dark hair danced wildly free of its immaculate setting and fell into tendrils on her forehead; silk snapped under his fingers and the left shoulder strap of her dress fell down.

"You sure aren't choosy about the weapons you use to hurt people when you can't get your own way, Ilena." Paul's eyes were like ice and the deep gully of a frown was etched above them. "Well, say what you like about me – I guess I'm the world's biggest sap as it is for putting up with you the way I do – but you can leave young Marny alone. She's just a kid, and I won't have her slandered by that reckless tongue of yours."

"Such anger! Such ice in your eyes for a *bon enfant*!" Ilena's lips and eyes spat rage at him, while the golden-gorse silk of her dress had slipped precariously. "A *bon enfant*!" She laughed maliciously. "From the look on your face, Paul, one might take her for your *belle amie*."

He looked then as though he could have struck Ilena. "You know damn well I haven't looked at another woman since we got engaged, but, by God," his eyes swept her from head to foot, "you're fast driving me to it with your crazy changes of mood. I begin to wonder lately whether I – oh, to hell with this!" He thrust her from him and flung out of the lounge, banging the hall door behind him with angry force. He didn't wait for the lift but went running down the stairs to the street. He was fuming as he climbed behind the wheel of his car and drove rapidly away from Routledge Court, making for a quiet club he knew of, where he could glower into several drinks and cool down after that nerve-racking scene with Ilena.

While he waited for some traffic signals to change he punched the wheel of the car. Damn her! What was she trying to do to him? A woman one minute, then the next a devil, a tigress, whom he had come dangerously close to striking.

It was fairly late when he arrived back at the Clinic, and after locking the front door he took a moody stroll through the grounds, where the trees rustled in the night air and the occasional hunting call of a tawny owl echoed weirdly. Here in the cool darkness Paul reviewed that disturbing scene with Ilena.

She wasn't sleeping well, he could see that for himself, and she had the worry of her cousin and their wedding on her mind. But all the same he found it hard forgiving her for those nasty allusions to rumours about Marny and himself.

He thought of Marny in his office that afternoon, barely suppressing her amusing urge to throw her arms about his neck so that she might hug him for wanting to adopt Ginger. She was little more than a child herself, and the things Ilena had said rankled rather bitterly. He was also darn sure that Nadia hadn't been gossiping about Marny behind her back. Nadia liked his young secretary. She had told him so only the other day.

Paul thrust his hands into the pockets of his dinner-jacket

and wandered back into the Clinic. Absorbed in his thoughts, he gave a start when the phone on the desk in his office began to ring. He plucked the receiver off the house-phone and heard Nurse Donkin on the line. Would he come up to number thirteen right away? Mrs. Barrington had a severe pain in her chest and she was breathing badly.

Paul had been worried about Ada for a week or more. She had lost a lot of her old cheerful zest just lately and a couple of times she had admitted to a pain in her chest. But she had obstinately refused to see a heart specialist colleague of Paul's.

"If the old ticker is wearing out at last, then let it wear out in peace," she had said to him. "I like it here at your Clinic, Paul, and you don't seem to mind having me."

He went flying up the stairs to her room, where he found the old queen of the music halls in a state of almost complete collapse. He was working fiercely with his nurses to try and revive the old lady when Ginger awoke in the room next door. The boy climbed out of bed and opened the door between his room and Ada's — a small, tousled figure in pyjamas, who stared petrified at the scene confronting him, bright light splashing Paul's white shirt and dark, intent face ... something that looked like a half-collapsed balloon over Ada's mouth.

Ginger began to cry, for kind Mrs. Barrington looked exactly like Billy Bennet's grandma had looked when she had fallen down in Barrow Street and they had brought her home and put her in a box in the parlour of Billy's house. Billy had let him have a look at her, and Ginger's sobs grew louder as he thought of Mrs. Barrington in a box like that one. . . .

In that moment Paul became aware of the boy's presence and he told one of the nurses to take him downstairs. "Phone over for Miss Lester," he added. "She'll look after him."

The nurse took hold of Ginger's hand and led him sobbing down to Paul's office, and it wasn't until Marny appeared that he grew a little calmer. The nurse told Marny that Mrs. Barrington had suffered a stroke, the gravity of her face added that there didn't seem much hope of the old lady pulling out of it. She then went back upstairs, and Marny sat in one of the big leather armchairs with Ginger in her arms.

Only that afternoon he had been in Ada's room and she had read several chapters of *Treasure Island* to him, making the pirate tale live for him with her colourful personality. Now he couldn't stop thinking of Billy Bennet's grandma, whose face had looked just like Ada's as he had just seen it, all fallen in and empty. He trembled and pressed against Marny, desperate for her feeling of aliveness, mystified and frightened by the way people you loved could suddenly stop being alive.

"You won't die, will you, Marny?" he whispered. "I don't like it when people die – they don't look like people any more."

She stroked his tousled hair and talked to him in a soft, comforting voice, explaining that when people grew old they grew tired and wanted to sleep. In that sleep they went home to God, so he mustn't ever be afraid of it.

The boy listened, hugging her fiercely with his young arms. He burrowed his tear-wet face inside her dressing-gown, so that his cheek was closer still to her warmth and the reassuring beat of her heart through her nightdress. He eventually fell asleep like that, and Marny wouldn't move for fear of disturbing him. The clock ticked steadily and a draught blew through the half-open door between the office and Paul's sitting-room. Tiger sat on his master's desk, watching Marny with the steady, knowing eyes of a cat, and her legs grew cold, her arms cramped about the sleeping child.

It was getting on for three o'clock when Paul came down to the office, looking haggard and defeated. He had been unable to save Ada. She had revived for a short while, then she had relapsed into a coma and quietly died.

Paul carefully took the sleeping boy out of Marny's arms. "Nurse Donkin has prepared him another room," he murmured. "I'll take him up."

Marny stood rubbing some life back into her cramped arms. "I'll go and make some coffee, Mr. Stillman. I expect you could do with a cup, couldn't you?"

"Yes, please, honey!"

They sat drinking coffee in his sitting-room, sadly talking about Ada, recalling her love of a good joke and the rich singing voice which she had never lost. When Marny rose to go back to the bungalow, Paul walked with her through the office to the glass doors. The dawn light was spilling chiffon-light over the grounds and the sparkle of dew was on the grass.

"It's helped me, Marny, talking to you," Paul said, and his arm slipped about her waist as they stood together in the open doors. She was touchingly small compared to him. Her head just reached the lapels of his white shirt and she felt slender as a wand in the hard circle of his arm. "Get a couple of hours' sleep," he smiled down at her.

"Yes . . ." She stood gazing up at him and neither of them actively willed what happened next, but suddenly both his arms were around her. He found her mouth almost blindly . . . sweet . . . God, how sweet! He had to expand all his pent-up emotions upon the soft mouth beneath his. The pain of his fight with Ilena, his grief at losing an old and valued friend.

Marny lay in his arms, lost on the wave of his urgency, but unafraid, letting him find the mental quietness he was in need of. He kissed her, turbulently, and she felt the hard, shaking

112

beat of his heart . . . then his sudden stillness as he came back to earth and realized what he was doing.

His arms dropped away from her and she saw a hot tide of blood mount under the skin of his throat and face.

"There's nothing I can say, Marny," he spoke thickly, contritely. "Apologies don't really lighten one's offences, they only seem to intensify them. I can only ask you very humbly to forget my behaviour just now."

She didn't speak, she just pressed his arm, and then she was gone, flitting across the grass as silently as the spreading daylight.

Marny didn't attend Ada Barrington's funeral.

It took place on Friday, and Paul gave Errol Dennis permission to drive Marny and Ginger down to Norfolk to visit her people. The main idea, of course, was to get Ginger away from the Clinic for the day. Ada's few remaining relatives lived in South Africa, and Paul had decided that as she had made a sort of second home of his Clinic, her funeral cars should leave from there.

Errol borrowed Alec Gordon's Austin for the day and they bowled along steadily, stopping in Newmarket for lunch so that Ginger might see some of the jockeys from the nearby racing stables and arriving in Norfolk about two o'clock.

Aunt Marjorie was overjoyed to see Marny, though she remarked at once she was looking thinner, and she made a great deal of Ginger.

Later on, when they had tea in the garden under one of the big lime trees, Marny grew amused by the little glances of speculation which her aunt kept shooting at Errol. He wore a smart dark blue suit and he looked both handsome and surprisingly respectable. He listened charmingly and attentively while Aunt Marjorie described a recent exciting yachting race on the Broads, and after tea he showed a genuine interest in the miniature cactus dahlias which had won Marny's aunt a first prize at a local flower show.

When Uncle Richard and Derek arrived home from work, Derek lost very little time getting Marny to himself.

He wanted to find out just how serious her intentions were regarding this "handsome Irish blighter in the cracking suit from Whitley's". He took Marny up to their old romping room at the top of the house and she sat on the old rocking-horse, whose fire was almost entirely extinguished, and talked to Derek about the Clinic, the patients, the absorbing interest she had developed in all of it.

"But what about this Irish chap?" Derek growled through his cigarette smoke. He considered that as a first cousin who had once been sweet on Marny himself he had the right to ap-prove or veto her choice of a prospective mate. Actually he was rather taken with Errol. The chap had been around, of course, anyone could see that, but he had a rather nice way of talking to Marny. She didn't seem to take much notice, it was true, but modern girls were never too ready to show what they felt for a chap.

"Errol?" she laughed, and rocked the old painted horse on which she sat. "Do you think he's the man who might rip my armour into small pieces?"

Derek studied his cousin. He agreed with his mother, Marny did look thinner, and that was usually a sign that a girl was in love.

"The armour isn't quite as intact as it was, my girl," Derek remarked.

Her green eyes widened, then she slipped off the rocking-horse and walked to the cupboard that held her childhood toys. She wanted Ginger to have some of them. The big teddy-bear

114

with one bent ear, a box of marbles, several games and her complete collection of the *William* books.

"Help me with these, Derry," she requested.

He came and took the pile of books out of her hands. "How do you get on with Paul Stillman?" he wanted to know.

"We get on fine."

"Is he a tough cookie?"

She blew the dust off a box of paints and put it on top of the books Derek was holding. "I suppose some people might consider him a bit intimidating," she said. "He looks tough, but underneath it he's very kind."

"Most men will want to be kind to you, little cousin," Derek laughed. "You've grown as pretty as paint since you've been away, do you know that?"

"Derry, you don't alter." She spoke with exasperation. "You need taking in hand by some nice girl, otherwise you're going to develop into a regular flirt."

"Like your Errol Dennis?" he enquired impudently.

Her cheeks flushed carnation-pink. "He isn't my Errol Dennis – what an idea!"

"I should imagine it's an idea that would appeal to most girls."

"Derry, you're incorrigible!" Marny stalked past her cousin with a big teddy-bear in her arms, and she heard him chuckling to himself as he followed her downstairs.

When Errol drove the Austin away from the house they also took with them at Aunt Marjorie's insistence a couple of giant marrows, an immense bunch of flowers and a big walnut cake.

"I like your people," Errol said, driving carefully past a family of ducks, taking a walk in the late afternoon sunshine. "Your aunt is especially nice; rather like the two aunts I have back in County Mayo. The two brave old dears brought me

115

up, and it's only now that I realize what a torment I was to them."

Marny smiled. "Aunt Marjorie thought you quite charming. She told me so."

Errol's tawny glance swept up and down Marny's profile. He seemed about to say something, then changed his mind and didn't say it until they reached the Clinic. They stood talking in the hall for a few minutes, then almost diffidently Errol asked Marny if she would go out dining and dancing with him the following evening.

It would have been ungracious to refuse him, after he had been such a charming companion all day, so Marny accepted the invitation.

"Sure now, that's grand of you, Marny. I'll call for you at eight o'clock." He smiled into her eyes, ruffled the sleepy Ginger's hair and said goodnight to them. Marny gazed after his slender figure and she wondered wildly for a moment whether she had been wise to say yes to him, then her thoughts were diverted from him as Scotty came across the hall, demanding to know how they had enjoyed their day in Norfolk.

Quite a lot of paper work had piled up in the office owing to Paul's preoccupation with Ada Barrington's funeral, and he and Marny were obliged to set to Saturday morning in an attempt to clear it out of the way. By twelve-thirty he had dictated his letters and he left Marny typing them while he went upstairs to the X-ray room to look at some plates. He called in to see Nadia after he left the X-ray room. He had not had a chance to talk to her for a couple of days and he wanted to ask her if there was something troubling Ilena which he didn't know about.

"I can't help admitting she's got me worried, Nadia," he said. "She seems so nervy and on edge lately. I know she's involved in a lot of gay plans for this wedding of ours, but this nerviness of hers is kind of contagious. The other evening the pair of us indulged in a pretty nasty quarrel."

"Paul," Nadia took his hand and drew him down on the side of her bed, "Ilena has always lived on her nerves. As a child she was so exquisite that people naturally made much of her. This was never a good thing. It has tended to make her – how shall I say it? – over-conscious of herself. She likes to be the centre of continual dramas, I am afraid."

Paul smiled a little. Nadia was five years younger than Ilena, and so many years older in wisdom.

"I know she's a spoilt brat, Nadia," he said bluntly, "but she said some things the other evening that got me pretty riled up. She – intimated that there's been some talk here at the Clinic about – well, about Marny and me."

"Marny – and you, Paul?" Nadia looked shocked. "But that is nonsense! Marny is not the kind of girl to encourage the attentions of men – least of all the attentions of a man betrothed to another girl. Ilena is unkind to say such a thing. She is more than unkind, she is cruel and unthinking. She does not deserve you at times, Paul."

He smiled wryly. "Oh, I'm no angel, Nadia, but when I came to the realization that I wanted a wife and I put a ring on Ilena's hand, I put a brake on my bachelor ways. Any man does, if he respects the bargain he's made with the woman he wants to marry, and it darn well hurt that Ilena should think I had gone back on our bargain – with young Marny."

Then all at once a flush stung his skin and he was remembering the way he had held and kissed Marny the other morning. She had yielded herself with a warm innocence, recognizing that he needed a little balm for his wounded feelings. Thank the lord it had been he who had needed the

117

balm and not someone with her interests less at heart!

He said to Nadia: "We've talked enough about my troubles, which will no doubt resolve themselves, and I've a bit of heartening news about René Blanchard."

"René?" Her fingers gripped Paul's and her tilted eyes dwelt upon his face in a pathetic eagerness. All awareness of what they had been talking about drained out of her and there was nothing but René ... René. "Tell me quickly!" she breathed.

"Well, your father was at Ilena's place the other evening, along with a Professor Dubois, who it seems was René's tutor at the Sorbonne. He managed to persuade the court that René is not really a violent man – just misguided – and he only received a moderate sentence."

"Are you saying that he will be put in a prison, Paul?"

"Yes, my dear."

"But prison!" Nadia's eyes grew haunted. "René has always been a man of action. How will he bear it, shut in by stone walls, without a horse to ride across the wild, free sands and the wind to sing against his skin? He will pine for his freedom like a caged eagle."

"Nadia," Paul gripped her hands and his eyes were silver bright, with a fighting light in them, "if René knows you're waiting for him, he'll bear the torment of his cage. He'll bear it with even greater heart if he knows you're fighting your own particular battle with everything you've got."

"You almost convince me that I should fight, Paul." She smiled tremulously and tears came into her eyes. "I love René so much – so much!"

"Then prove what you feel for him," Paul urged. "Have confidence in yourself and in my judgment. If your legs were helpless, Nadia, I'd tell you so. I wouldn't ask you to fight a battle you could never win. Look at me, my dear," he tipped her face to him and felt her tears roll down over his fingers. "Have you forgotten the afternoon you were spilled out of your chair? You were afraid Marny had been hurt and you made yourself get back into your chair so that you could get to her. You weren't thinking about yourself, honey. You weren't telling yourself it wasn't worth the effort to find out whether your friend had been hurt. You had a reason for what you did – surely you have a greater one where René is concerned?"

"What must I do?" she whispered.

"Come to the gym and prove to yourself that you can stand up."

"I – stand up?" She looked ironical, yet eager.

He smiled, the quick, charming smile which Marny liked so much. "With the help of supports, naturally, but once you've felt the ground under your feet again, you'll begin to fight to have it there without the aid of supports. The fighting will hurt, Nadia. It'll rack the muscles you haven't used for such a long time, but the pain will be worthwhile."

" 'Suffer in order to know; toil in order to have.' " Then she smiled a little. "I think I have always known that you'd have your way in the end."

She held out her arms to him, and he lifted her feather-light figure out of the bed, gently buttoned her into a dressing-gown and carried her to the gymnasium.

It was a moment of triumph which they both wanted to share with Marny, and Paul phoned down for her. She came up to the gym at once, and her face crinkled with delight when she found that Paul had at last persuaded Nadia to try her legs.

He was holding her while she balanced herself on a pair of metallic supports that somewhat resembled those used by ballet dancers when they are practising their steps. "Careful!" he murmured. "There, now your feet are on the ground!" Slowly, carefully he withdrew his arms from Nadia and she stood alone between the supports, a thin, trembling, yet triumphant figure, whom Paul left in Marny's charge when he was suddenly called away to another patient. Nadia was to have fifteen minutes in the gym, no more, he warned. Her practice doses would be increased gradually, for they mustn't overtax the muscles she had not used for two years.

Nadia gallantly propelled herself backwards and forwards between the metal rails. Each cumbersome movement was for René's sake, and this gave her heart, though the perspiration was soon trickling down her back, while her arms and legs were crying out a protest. When her fifteen minutes were up, Marny fetched her chair and wheeled her to the bathroom, where Nadia soaked in a warm tub in tired but elated comfort while Marny sat on a linen-basket and talked about her day at Norfolk with Ginger and Errol.

"He is a very handsome young man," Nadia lazily murmured, her eyes upon the wriggle of her own toes in the soapy water. Happiness squeezed her throat and she welcomed the aching muscles that proclaimed her victory over her helplessness. "Yes, Mr. Dennis is exceedingly chic," she repeated, her glance lifting mischievously to Marny's face. "He is like a faun, I think. So slender and graceful, and I should imagine he likes to do a great deal of kissing."

"Nadia — really!" Marny exclaimed. "He was as good as gold all day yesterday. He knows there's to be nothing like that when I go out with him."

"Poor young man!" Nadia's tilted eyes were gleaming with laughter. "To think he does not know that tonight he will be dancing with an icicle in his arms."

"Shut up!" Marny snatched the sponge out of the bath and squeezed a deluge of soapy water over Nadia's head.

When Marny eventually returned to the office a surprise awaited her in elegant form of Ilena Justine. She was standing by the open glass doors with a cigarette in her hand. She looked incredibly smart in a red cloche hat and a black sheath dress worn with a lovely string of pearls.

"Good morning, Miss Justine!" Marny smiled and sat down at her typewriter. "You'll be pleased to hear that Nadia has just been trying her legs in the gym. Mr. Stillman is terribly pleased with her."

Ilena watched Marny for a moment, her almond-shaped eyes taking in the little white blouse and dark green skirt that made of Marny a fragile, snowdrop figure. Her bright hair did not detract from the illusion; she seemed a snowdrop in a ray of sunshine.

She glanced up, feeling the other girl's scrutiny, and Ilena came to her desk with that seductive, tip-toe walk of hers, induced by the incredibly high heels of her red shoes.

"How long have you been at the Clinic?" she asked.

Marny glanced at the desk calendar. "Just on three months."

"You are fond of your job, no?"

"Yes, it's a very worthwhile job, Miss Justine."

"Worthwhile, eh?" Ilena lifted her cigarette, drew on it and slowly expelled the smoke through tiny, chiselled nostrils. She didn't really think for a moment that there was anything going on between Paul and this girl, but the extent of his indignation the other evening had been revealing. It had proved that he wasn't entirely blind to the girl's attractiveness, and Ilena knew that a woman's attractions assume even greater significance to a man when they are accompanied by a sympathetic attitude. Marny Lester's sympathetic attitude had to be dealt with. She must be shown that even crumbs from Paul's table were prohibited. Paul belonged to *her*, Ilena.

"*Chérie*," Ilena said softly, "may I offer you a piece of advice?" She leant a hand on the desk and her delicate, expensive perfume wafted to Marny.

Marny gazed back at the French girl and sudden antagonism was active in her again. She felt it, like a bitter taste at the back of her mouth. Ilena was lovely ... incredibly so in her own exotic way ... but she repelled Marny, and the younger girl had to fight to remain seated, so close to the almond eyes that shimmered, so within range of the scarlet fingernails that stretched taut like weapons.

"Advice, Miss Justine?" she queried.

"Yes, it is this. Paul is naturally pleased with your efficiency here in the office, but he does not wish you to get personally involved in his life. He prefers that businesslike relationship be maintained between you at all times – you comprehend? He would not say this to you himself. He would not wish to hurt your feelings, but I think it is better that you be told."

"But," Marny was looking bewildered, "I don't quite know what you're getting at."

"Oh, come!" Ilena laughed delicately. "My fiancé was recently foolish to show an interest in you which was hardly very employer-like. He is sorry now. He feels that you might have misconstrued his interest – as we shall call it."

Every particle of colour drained out of Marny's face. She remembered Paul kissing her, here in this office the other morning, and she experienced a severe shock of revulsion. How could he have told Ilena about that! How could he!

Ilena went on: "Paul, like most warm-hearted men, is often a victim of his impulses. He feels sometimes troubled about

122

you because you are alone in London, but I should not impose on this if I were you." The petrol-blue eyes searched out the pain and the wounded pride in the pale young face raised to them, and Ilena knew she had drawn blood. With calculated intention she dipped her claws in Marny's blood. "You are little more than a child, but children sometimes want the possessions of others, therefore they must be rapped on the knuckles before their desire gets too strong for them and they commence to steal. Paul is too soft-hearted to do his own rapping when it comes to – children, but I have not this drawback."

Then Ilena turned with feline grace from Marny's desk, for footsteps suddenly approached the door and Paul walked into the office.

He stared when he saw his fiancé.

"Hullo, daarling!" She dotted her cigarette in Marny's ashtray, then walked across to Paul with outstretched hands. She blinked her jetty eyelashes at him and he saw that she wore the pearls he had recently given her. A token of surrender, he wryly thought. A symbolic means of saying "Forgive me . . . let there be peace between us!" And he accepted her into his arms, for sooner or later they had to make up their quarrel, but he didn't miss the way Marny averted her head from them as she approached the filing cabinet.

"Daarling, take me to lunch." Ilena made herself small and coaxing in his arms. "You are looking a little frayed about the edges. You work too hard – give too much of yourself to this place."

Yes, he did feel rather frayed about the edges, and for once he welcomed the thought of getting away from the Clinic for a while, into the elegant atmosphere of a West End restaurant where Ilena would just look lovely and talk him into forgetting their quarrel of the other evening. He glanced across at Marny. "You can go to lunch yourself, Marny," he said. "I shan't need you any more today."

"Very well, Mr. Stillman."

She didn't look round until the door of his sitting-room closed, then she realized that she was trembling, so much that she had to sit down. Then for several long moments she gazed unseeingly at Paul's desk, a hand crushed against her mouth. She felt bruised ... used. She would have given anything to be able to wipe out the memory of having yielded herself to Paul as she had done. She had thought him in pain, and in need, and it hadn't seemed wrong in the dawn light, with the sparkle of dew on the grass, to let him kiss her.

Her mouth ached again, but with a more terrible pain than that induced by the kisses which she had answered.

She quivered, like a creature stung. Yes, she had answered them ... clenched her hands against the hard muscles of Paul's back, while the world tilted for a precarious moment and desire ... her desire ... met the man's.

Marny finally got to her feet. She tidied the office automatically, then walked slowly across the grounds to the bungalow. Now she hated it here at the Clinic. She could barely face the thought of remaining until Ginger had undergone his operation, which was scheduled for the coming Wednesday.

CHAPTER VII

ERROL was waiting in the hall of the Clinic when Marny came through the entrance which the nurses always used. Her hair was swirled back in a shining French knot, leaving her temples hollowed and young. Tiny topaz drops swung in the lobes of her ears and her evening gown was a lovely champagne colour. Over her gown she wore a short fur jacket, and she had a cool, fresh loveliness this evening that was somehow intensified by the deep, almost haunted jade green of her eyes.

"You rare female!" Errol was looking strikingly handsome in his evening clothes. "It's exactly eight o'clock and you're all dressed and ready for me." Then he handed her a small plastic box. "I hope you like roses."

She opened the box and discovered a pair of close-furled, honey-yellow roses nestling on several dainty fronds of fern. "How lovely!" She was genuinely pleased and touched that he should give her the roses.

"Let me pin them on for you." They stood close together as he pinned the roses to the collar of her jacket, then he led her out to the taxi-cab he had waiting. He was taking her to the Orchid Club for dinner and West End parking problems had made him dispense with his car tonight. They climbed into the cab and he gave her destination to the driver. Then as the cab moved out from the kerb and they settled themselves, Errol said: "You look a peach tonight, Marny. I've never seen you look lovelier."

She flushed slightly and her green eyes met his tawny ones.

She caught her breath a little, for his eyes weren't afire, dominating and male. They were curiously gentle, while his mouth held that hint of sweetness which she had always thought was in his nature. His mouth mesmerised her when he added softly, "You're a dear, gallant little kid, aren't you?"

Since her painful conversation with Ilena at lunchtime, Marny had been feeling raw and bruised. Now Errol looked at her with his Irish face kindling into a dark beauty ... his glance caressed and comforted her. She returned his smile, and did not reject his warm fingers when they closed on hers.

The Orchid Club was renowned for its glamorous décor, its exciting orchestra and excellent cuisine. Errol was obviously a regular patron here, for their waiter addressed him by name as he led them to a table beside the dance floor. The waiter whisked a reserved notice off the table, and his dark Italian eyes rested on Marny with appreciation as Errol removed her jacket and the topaz shoulder-straps of her gown glittered against her fresh young skin and her hair shone under the chandeliers of the restaurant.

"What do you recommend, Nino?" Errol enquired, after Marny had signified that he choose their meal. He and the waiter consulted together over the menu, and the meal they finally decided on was delicious and accompanied by a sparkling Barsac that made Marny pleasantly woozy.

They danced, and Errol talked charming Irish nonsense, so that by the time they left the Orchid Club Marny was smilingly relaxed, receptive to his arm within hers as they strolled along the Strand and turned down towards the Embankment. A full moon shed its silver down on the water, and Errol saw twin moons reflected in Marny's green eyes when they paused by the parapet.

"Had fun?" he asked.

"Yes. You're a very good dancer, Errol," she smiled.

"I hope you aren't thinking it's because I've had plenty of practice?"

"No – no – "

"No?" He laughed at her, but gently. Then she heard him give a sigh as he leant his arms upon the parapet; he stared down towards the trembling, silver-starred water. "I guess I do play around," he admitted. "I gamble, too, for kicks and money – oh, Marny, why did you have to come into my life? You've forced me to develop a conscience, and the bad things I do no longer give me any pleasure. I – I'm caught in a kind of vacuum. I want to be a better person than I have been – but why should it be for nothing?"

Marny regarded him with troubled eyes. She half-conceived what he was getting at, and a tremor of uncertainty shook her. The girl in her wanted to run from him; the woman felt him reaching out, begging a little mercy of her, and it was the woman in her that asked : "What do you want of me, Errol?"

He turned to look at her, and she saw that his face had a sudden drawn look. "I want you, Marny," he said.

She drew back from him, the moonlight shimmering on her hair and showing the jade of her eyes, the fragile whiteness of her throat.

"I see." She spoke calmly enough, but her heart was racing. "I – I'm afraid I don't go in for promiscuous love affairs, Errol."

She heard him catch his breath. "You think I'm asking that of you?" he exclaimed.

"Aren't you?"

"Darlin', no!" His wiry fingers found hers and gripped them. "I must be a pretty low specimen in your eyes if you think I'm asking you to be promiscuous. You! Why, don't

127

you know that I could be an angel for love of someone like you?"

She stared at him, looking young and lost. Then he had drawn her hands to his lips. A moment afterward she was in his arms and his broken murmurs were lost in her hair.

"Little Marny – little breakable thing!" he whispered. "I feel clean again, just being near you. God, how I've wanted to feel clean again, like the wind over the green hills of Ireland – green like your eyes."

The shaken deluge of words left Marny defenceless, with no way of rejecting and hurting him. There was also a strange comfort in being wanted as much as Errol seemed to want her.

Going home in a cab he began talking about rings. Talking fast, as though he didn't want to give her time to think. When they reached the Clinic he held her in his arms at the door. "Marry me soon," he begged, "for it's a lonely man I am. Lonelier than you think."

His cry that he was lonely touched Marny to the heart, for she had known some aching bouts of loneliness herself since the death of her parents. "I know what it feels like to be lonely," she said.

"Darlin', it turns a man to the devil himself!"

She gently touched his face, felt the fine modelling of the bones that always gave him the medieval look of a man in a Florentine painting. He stood quietly under the shy touch of her fingers, for he had learned long ago that women liked to touch his face. He had accepted it, but it hadn't meant much beyond that his handsome face got him what he wanted. But this was different! He thrilled to the exploration of Marny's fingers, their cool wandering down over his cheekbones until they reached the chiselled perfection of his mouth.

"Well?" he murmured.

"You have the face of an acient Greek. You're a disgustingly handsome thing, Errol."

He laughed and nuzzled his face in her hair. "Good. We'll be the best-looking couple that ever signed a marriage register."

"Oh, I'm quite mediocre," she protested. "Probably the only woman I know who could really match you for looks is Ilena Justine."

He went strangely still, then his arms closed painfully hard about Marny's slight figure. "Don't let's talk about other people," he said raggedly. "Don't let's even think about them."

"Errol —" His intensity frightened her and she tried to pull away from him.

Then a cockchafer whirred out of a nearby tree. Marny jumped as the large wings of the creature brushed her hair and the movement impelled her back against Errol. He captured her mouth; when he let her go she turned blindly from him and fled into the Clinic.

It was Julie Brelson's birthday the following day, and in the evening the nurses had a small party over at the bungalow.

"I could hear the crowd of you having a darn good time," Paul said to Marny, on Monday morning.

"I hope we didn't disturb you," she said.

"Not at all. I always enjoy your playing, Marny."

He began to read his morning's mail, and Marny glanced up from her typewriter when he gave a small exclamation of surprise. "Say, I've got a letter here from Ada Barrington's solicitors," he told her. "D'you know what that great old girl has done? She's left five thousand pounds to young Ginger. It seems that the codicil was only recently added to her will, and she's named me as Ginger's executor."

"How marvellous of her!" Marny forgot some of her constraint with Paul. She hurried round his desk and read the letter with him, which went on to say that Mrs. Barrington wanted the child to be sent to a good school, and later on there would be enough money to enable him to study for a career.

"If Nell Farning gets to hear about this she'll fight to have the boy home with her," Paul said. "But, by God, she isn't going to have him!" He tapped the letter. "This, Marny, has got to be kept to ourselves until after the operation, then with the worry of it off my mind I'll be in a better state to fight that creature. Say, to think dear old Ada should do such a swell thing. It's real good of her, isn't it?"

"I've never heard of anything so kind." Marny was standing close to Paul, and he wrapped an arm about her waist, almost without thinking. Then he glanced up at her.

"How much do you weigh?" he enquired.

"Why – about eight stone."

"You're very thin, child." His eyes travelled over her with a sudden professional speculation. "You're more near seven stone than eight. Are you eating properly?"

"Of course." She attempted to withdraw from his arm, but immediately it tightened.

"Marny, you're not looking well. Is there anything troubling you? Are you worrying about Ginger, maybe?"

"Yes." She clutched at the excuse. "Yes, I suppose I am worrying."

"Well, another couple of days and it will all be over. You're going to the Chardmore Ball tonight, aren't you? Swell! The gaiety and the dancing will take your mind off the operation for a while." He released her, and she returned to her desk. After a moment or two he glanced up from a second perusal of the letter concerning Ginger, and he was smiling slightly. "By the way, what are you going as? I shall want to have a dance with you. I know you're going to look very lovely."

Marny couldn't look at him, for she had flushed to the roots of her red hair with resentment. She didn't want his compliments; she wanted their relationship kept strictly on that businesslike basis which Ilena had talked about. "Did you want codeine added to this list of supplies, Mr. Stillman?" she asked stiffly.

"Eh – codeine? Yes, you might as well put it on. The usual quantity." He studied her briefly over the top of a letter, aware that her mood was jumpy and unreceptive this morning. He thought he knew the cause, and he was trying hard to show her that things were back on their old footing between them, that she didn't have to fear he'd ever touch her again. "Now come on," he wheedled, "tell me what kind of a forest creature you'll be impersonating at this sylvan evening of Lady Chardmore's?"

"I'm going as a dragonfly," she rubbed out a mistyped word, frowning as she smudged her carbon copy. "Nadia lent me the costume."

"That was nice of Nadia. You two get on well, don't you"

"Yes, I like Nadia. She's a nice person. She deserves to have things come right for her."

"Well, things look a lot brighter all round. Blanchard will be bound to be given a short prison sentence."

Marny stopped typing, abruptly. "But what about the awful gang of louts who are still throwing bombs left, right and centre? They tried to kill René Blanchard outside the Santé prison a couple of weeks ago. Suppose they try again?"

Paul tapped a finger thoughtfully against his bottom lip. "There's a chance that they will, I agree, but from newspaper accounts, the student riots seem to be dying down." Then he frowned slightly as he regarded her. "I had no idea you knew about that Santé prison business? Nadia doesn't know, does she?"

Marny shook her head. "Miss Justine told me about the bombing raid when I went over to her flat the other Sunday to collect Nadia's costume."

"I didn't know you'd ever been to Ilena's flat." He sounded quite surprised.

Marny looked at him with equal surprise. "It was the Sunday Miss Justine returned from Paris," she explained, taking it for granted that he knew Ilena had returned on the Sunday.

"Marny, you're getting your days mixed up," he laughed. "Ilena came home from Paris on a Monday. I particularly remember because I had a talk with Martin Stein that same evening about a patient of mine at the Stepney Memorial, and I called in on Ilena after I left the Steins' place."

For a moment Marny was dumbfounded by what he said. Words of denial were trembling on her lips, and then some peculiar sixth sense seemed to tell her not to give voice to them. "H-how silly of me," she managed to smile, as though at her own forgetfulness. "It was on a Monday, I remember now."

But as they talked on, mental pictures of Ilena's strange manner that Sunday afternoon were crowding back into Marny's mind, distracting her thoughts from what Paul was saying, something about transferring his Stepney Memorial patient here to the Clinic for more extensive treatment. Marny remembered Ilena's near-hysteria that afternoon, the drawn tenseness of her face as she had said: "– Be discreet. Do not mention that I am home today – to anyone."

To anyone? She had meant Paul, of course. Therefore she

had been trumping up a story when she had said she had left Paris early because of that bombing raid. If she could tell Marny she had come home because of the raid, she could tell Paul. Marny pressed the back of her right hand against her mouth and she was hardly aware that she bit her knuckles. That scarlet car in the mews of Routledge Court came rushing into her mind. Upholstered in dove-grey leather and so much like Errol's . . . so frighteningly like Errol's!

"– Martin agrees with me that there seems some hope of restoring Sacha's hands to a partial use," Paul was saying, dragging her thoughts back from Routledge Court, where the sun had streamed hot through the windows and there had been something queer about the atmosphere of Ilena's flat; something you couldn't pin down, making you impatient to get away, out into the fresh air.

Marny's eyes fled to Paul, she caught at what he was saying, drew the affairs of the Clinic over her mind like a shield. "Sacha?" she said. "The man who used to make violins?"

Paul nodded. "Of course, he'll never be able to make his violins again, but we may in time make it possible for him to fashion less intricate things, such as toys, ashtrays, cigarette-boxes. Anyway, it's worth a try." Paul put down the letter-opener he had been playing with and got to his feet. As he came round his desk, he flexed his arms and gave a yawn that wasn't one of tiredness, but one of restlessness. Like the yawn of a big, prowling cat, Marny thought, as he strolled to the glass doors, stood there a moment, then walked over to her chair. She felt him behind her, felt him throughout her body, so that she hammered the wrong keys of her typewriter and was glad when he decided to make his rounds and walked from the room.

He spent some time with Ginger, who was missing Ada

Barrington, and in the end he took the boy along to see Nadia. He left him sitting on Nadia's bed, listening to a story, and as he walked to the X-ray room, where he wanted to discuss some plates with Errol, Paul found himself suddenly depressed by the barrier Marny was erecting between them. As an engaged man, and her employer, he should never have touched her. Now their friendship was spoiled, and he flinched anew as he thought of the way she had shrunk from him when he and stood behind her chair.

He entered the X-ray room, where Errol was cheerfully whistling as he worked, and right away Paul's eyes settled on the drifting smoke of a cigarette that lay on the edge of a saucer cn Errol's bench. Paul angrily ground it out. "You know damn well I don't allow any smoking near all this inflammable stuff," he snapped.

"Sorry, I'm sure." Errol pulled a face. He hadn't been expecting Paul this early, having forgotten that he wanted to discuss the plates he had brought back from the Stepney Memorial the other day. They discussed the plates, reached a mutual verdict concerning them, and Errol said: "You're operating on Ginger Farning this Wednesday, aren't you? Marny was telling me over dinner Saturday evening that you've got the mother's consent. A bit of a hard nut, eh?"

"Aren't they always?"

"You tell me," Errol quipped. "I'm only a lad."

"There is something I'll tell you." Paul's eyes flickered coldly over the coin-clear profile beside him. "Marny's a nice child. If you're dating her, I'd advise you to remember it."

"You employ her, old man, you don't own her," Errol drawled, insolently snapping his rubber gloves as he put them on. "Anyway, you can rest easy about my intentions, they're strictly honourable."

"Meaning?" Paul turned from the bench to look at Errol, his pupils dark and sharp in contrast to the light grey irises of his eyes.

"Meaning that I intend to marry her."

"You must be out of your mind!" Paul exclaimed. "Marny – why, she's the kind of girl who would want her marriage to last a lifetime, not a few wild months."

"You seem to know her very well," Errol rejoined, "but I know what she's like to hold and kiss. Twenty years of doing both wouldn't be enough." His face was suddenly naked with re-awakened hunger for Marny, for the slightness of her against him and the soft, untutored feel of her mouth. Paul read his face, and he was filled with revolt, hating the idea that Marny could entertain this man and want him. There was no denying his physical attractivness, but he was as promiscuous as a damn honey-bee. He flitted from woman to woman, took what he wanted and went gaily on his way again. Marny was young, but she was no fool. She must know all this about Errol.

"You're thinking I'm not a quarter good enough for her, aren't you, Stillman?" Errol's tawny eyes dwelt with sudden melancholy on Paul's face. "Some men aren't, till they marry, but won't you believe that I mean to do my darnedest to live up to Marny? Won't you believe that I know she's the sweetest thing that ever drew breath and that I'm still pinching myself to make sure I'm not just dreaming that I've got her – that she's mine?"

Paul turned back to the frame holding the X-ray plates. He peered at them, forcing himself to be objective, as a mere employer should be. "I'm glad, at least, that you appreciate your luck," he said. "Marny's a fine girl."

"She's a darlin'!" Errol smiled, young and carefree again

as he went to the other side of the room and began to develop a series of X-rays he had taken the day before.

The enormous garden of the Chardmore house looked like a fairyland that evening. Coloured lanterns swayed among the branches of the trees and strings of glittering lights stretched down to the water's edge, for the house overlooked the Thames.

The outdoor, colonnaded pavilion where the dancing was taking place reassumed its gay, Georgian air as it gradually filled up with masked figures in all manner of fantastic array. A great glistening witch-ball, suspended high in the centre of the pavilion ceiling, threw its rainbow facets down over the excited crowd, where bats danced with witches, elves flirted with butterflies, and willow trees sipped punch with wild flowers.

Paul was enjoying a drink with Martin Stein's wife while Ilena danced with Martin.

"How beautiful she looks!" Ruth said, admiringly watching Ilena in her silver costume. It clung like water to her lovely body, and she could indeed have been a sylph, carried up out of the oceanic depths by Poseidon's golden chariot so that she might mingle with mere mortals for this one night. Then Ruth glanced at Paul and she saw that he was not watching Ilena, but a girl, dressed as a dragonfly, who was just coming off the floor with Alec Gordon. They were laughing as they came towards the buffet table and Alec was saying, apologetically: "I'm afraid I'm a terrible dancer, Marny. If I've crippled you, I'll have to see about giving you some osteopathic treatment."

"Oh, you weren't as bad as all that," she laughingly protested. "It's that crowded floor." They reached the buffet table,

136

where she at once became aware of Paul. Their eyes met through their masks, and Paul saw her mouth move in the faintest of smiles as he spoke to her and introduced her to Ruth Stein. Alec was already acquainted with Ruth, for he had been employed by Paul since the Clinic had first been opened and Paul had known the Steins since his training days under Sir Austin Orde. Alec fetched strawberry ices for Marny and himself and the four of them stood talking.

Ruth Stein was in her early forties. She was a gynaecologist, a small, energetic person who made entertaining gestures with her hands as she talked and whose bobbed, silver-threaded hair contrasted rather oddly with the squirrel costume she was wearing. She had removed the headpiece because she said it made her hot. Her clever, monkeyish face crinkled a smile at Marny as she complimented her on the dragonfly costume. It had needed only a few minor alterations. These had been obligingly tackled by Nurse Donkin, who was rather more deft with her needle than Marny was, and now the costume fitted Marny as though she had been born wearing it. It glittered and twinkled as she moved, while the globes on her cap kept blinking like little red eyes. Charming and absurd, Paul thought, as his mask-shadowed eyes moved over her.

"Paul's a devil, he'll never dress up properly for these occasions," Ruth scolded.

Paul laughed and tucked into a Danish sandwich, for the buffet table was amply supplied with a mixture of appetizing-looking eatables. He was dressed coolly and simply in breeches and a plaid shirt; a dash of Canadian forests clung about him. "Dressing up, Ruth, is for decorative creatures like you women. Don't you agree with me, Alec?"

Alec, looking hot and uncomfortable in a white druid's gown, was in heartfelt agreement with this sentiment. He had

137

let Errol persuade him into coming to this dance, but now he was here, he was heartily wishing he was at home attending to the tropical fish which he bred in a specially heated shed in the garden of his mother's house. Here, foolishly dressed up, he felt like a fish out of water.

"Where's Errol?" Paul enquired of Marny. Errol was dancing with Julie, and Marny pointed him out. She watched Paul's eyes grow quizzical behind his mask as he surveyed Errol, who had come as a devil. He was entirely in black and there were horns on his head, while a forked tail swung from the back of his tights. "He looks like old Nick!" Paul remarked, with a cynical twist to his mouth.

"He's wicked and beautiful," Ruth Stein said, following Errol with her eyes. Only Paul saw the vivid blush that crept to the edges of Marny's green mask. Then quite suddenly, the orchestra swung into a foxtrot, and Marny felt her heart turn over in panic as Paul said to Ruth Stein: "Will you excuse me, Ruth? It's about time I had a dance with my secretary." His fingers encircled Marny's wrist and she couldn't protest against dancing with him, not in front of Ruth and Alec. She had to let him lead her on to the crowded floor, where of necessity he had to hold her close to him to save her from being bumped too much. But he knew she was unrelaxed. She followed his steps like a little automaton, and a sudden anger shook him that she should behave like this. He gathered her head against him, and immediately he felt the taut resentment of her body, the little heave of her breasts, then the sudden giving in to his strength, the melting against him, into him. They danced silently until the music ceased, then he saw that they had drawn level with one of the archways that led directly to the river and he said to her. "Let's get out of this swarm. I feel like a fish in an overcrowded tank."

"No –" She pulled back from him, but he didn't intend to be denied. He led her from the pavilion, out into the night. It was cool and coloured lights spangled their path to the river, where Paul suggested they sit down on a rustic seat. "Cigarette?" He extended his case and his eyes smiled as the tiny globes on her cap kept flickering on and off. "I agree with Ruth," he murmured, "your costume is delightful. It suits you."

"Thank you." She watched the smoke of their cigarettes mingle in the air, listened to the nightjars as they hunted the ghost-moths that haunted the willows at the water's edge.

"Look, Marny, aren't we pals any more?" Paul asked. "Have I ruined everything so completely?"

"I thought we were pals," her heart cried out, while she sat silently, not answering him. She had nothing to answer him with.

"Marny," he leant forward and his left hand found hers and gripped it, "the other morning I was feeling darned miserable about Ada, and about something else, and – and you were there being so sweet to me. What I did was wrong, and I'm deeply ashamed, but please don't hate me for being – well, for being a blasted man, I suppose."

"The whole thing has got out of proportion." She jerked her hand free of his and she spoke coldly, unable to forget Ilena's hints that she was intruding into Paul's life; that he was worried in case she had misconstrued any interest which he might have shown in her. "The matter was forgotten by me the moment I left you that morning and returned to the bungalow. But I'd like you to know that a businesslike attitude in the office, and out of it, suits me fine."

"When did you reach that decision?" he asked. "Or did someone reach it for you – Errol Dennis, perhaps?"

"Errol?" Her hand jerked, spilling cigarette ash, and her eyes raced over Paul's face, which was suddenly all grim mouth and hard, cleft chin below the dark mask. "Errol has got nothing to do with this."

"He's the man you're marrying, isn't he?"

"Have you any objection?" she flashed. "If you have, then I consider that you're being officious. You're intruding into *my* private life."

Paul watched her, hurt, mystified, at a loss to understand why they had suddenly become strangers who wanted to wound one another with painful words. "No, your life is your own," he said. "I shouldn't dream of intruding into it and dictating to you, but I can't forget our friendship as easily as you seem able to. We were friends, Marny. Why, only the other day we were talking together about Ginger and you were as happy as a little lark about my plan to adopt him. What's happened to change your attitude so drastically towards me?"

"I don't want you to think that I expect to be treated as a friend," she replied. "I'm just your secretary. You don't have to confide in me and t-tell me your private plans. I'd sooner not hear about them. I-I prefer that our relationship be kept strictly on a businesslike basis."

"Marny," he leant towards her, suddenly remembering Ilena's allusion to rumours about Marny and himself; suddenly aware that there might have been some talk and that Marny was feeling hurt by it, "has there been any gossip about us at the Clinic?"

She gazed back at him with cold green eyes. "No, Mr. Stillman, there's been no gossip. Why, did you think I was so thrilled at being kissed by my *boss* that I couldn't wait to brag about it, over at the bungalow?"

"Marny!" His mouth was wounded. "What a hell of a thing

140

to say!'"

"Perhaps." She looked away from him and her chin was quivering. "But can you blame me for saying it? I'm a little country cousin ... I might make the mistake of thinking that men kiss for the same reason women do. Only you may rest assured that I don't. I might be a country girl, Mr. Stillman, but I'm not a congenital idiot. I do happen to know a little about men, and I also happen to respect the fact that you're engaged." Her cigarette glowed, and now she met his eyes. "You have no need to worry that I ever misconstrued your kisses or – or anything else."

"My worry, Marny, has been that you might think I had no respect for you, kissing you like some wild boy, with no thought for your feelings in the matter. My God, do you think I make a habit of grabbing my secretaries in dark corners?" He glanced away from her. "I'm an engaged man and I must have been out of my mind that morning, but I didn't mean to make you hate me."

She regarded his averted profile with bleak eyes, then she rose to her feet and walked to the river's edge, where tall rushes whispered together and the willows trailed their green tresses in the water, dappled by moonlight and the twinkling fairy globes. A few water-lilies floated lazily on their saucer-like leaves, their petals furled closely like the pallid lids of sleeping eyes. Marny heard the crunch as Paul walked towards the path that led back to the pavilion.

He threaded his way through the noisy crowd, thrusting the gay, entangling streamers from him, fighting free of a laughing circle of sprites, imps and owls. This was free-for-all night, when the lowliest student nurse, from behind a shielding mask could beg a dance of the loftiest chief resident.

"Come on, you lovely man, dance with me," a girlish voice

141

entreated Paul from behind a blackbird mask.

"Some other time, honey." He threw off her restraining hand and strode on towards the spot where he had stood in conversation with Ruth Stein. He found her husband there with several medical friends. They were talking shop, and Paul joined in until Ilena came to claim him for a dance.

Her eyes were excited and there were faint but lovely flushes on her high cheekbones. "The maddest young medical student has just given me a drink of vodka out of his flask and my head is whirling, Paul – whirling!" She urged him on to the crowded floor, where she felt naked in his arms in her silver costume. She pressed against him, touching the close-clipped hair at the nape of his neck. "Where have you been for the last half hour?" she demanded.

"Smoking a cigarette down by the river."

They circled the floor, bumping into other couples and getting entangled in balloons and streamers. Then Errol Dennis danced past with a slender, dragonfly figure held close against his black devil's costume. Ilena's eyes followed the couple. "Your little secretary appears to be enjoying herself with Mr. Dennis," she remarked.

"Why not?" Paul's mouth was cynical below his mask. "He informed me earlier on today that he intends to marry her."

The coloured witch-ball spun dizzily above Ilena ... the noise of the dance seemed to increase in volume ... then all at once she slumped unconscious in Paul's arms.

CHAPTER VIII

RUTH STEIN came out of the drawing-room of the Chardmore house, where Ilena was resting after her faint. She saw Paul sitting on a high-backed settle in the hall; he was unaware of her for a moment, the smoke of his cigarette wreathing up about his grey, abstracted eyes, from which he had now stripped his party mask. Ruth thought he looked rather unhappy. He had, she realized, looked that way all the evening. She approached him and he turned his head towards her. He rose from the settle.

"How is she, Ruth?" he asked.

"Much better, my dear." Ruth pressed his arm. "I should take her home, though, if I were you. She's had sufficient excitement for one evening."

"But what the devil made her faint, Ruth?" He thrust his boyish lock of hair back from his troubled eyes. "There isn't anything seriously wrong with her, is there?"

"Of course not. She's run down and she doesn't rest as much as she should. I've asked her to come to my consulting-rooms tomorrow morning, where I'll give her a thorough check-up. I rather think she's suffering from an iron deficiency, which should be put right." Ruth hesitated a moment, then she said: "Look, Paul, why don't you get married straight away and ensure that she does rest more?"

"Ilena wants the tomfoolery of a big fancy wedding," he rejoined, rather curtly. "We're almost in September, so I guess we might as well wait the full time."

"H'm –" Ruth's fingers played with the cuff of his plaid

shirt, and she wondered if Paul fully understood his fiancée's temperament. Ilena wanted a big fancy wedding – most girls did – but Ruth felt it would have been much more advisable for Paul to have insisted on a short engagement and a quick wedding. Ilena needed him far more than she fully understood herself, and Ruth, who dealt so closely with women, was surprised that the exquisite, highly-strung French girl had held out this long without her nerves giving way under the strain of waiting for Paul until October.

"Does it suit you to wait until October, Paul?" Ruth asked.

"As a matter of fact it does," he admitted bluntly. "We're pretty busy at the Clinic right now, and I've also been consulting an architect about adding a new wing. I want it for children only. At the moment I have to put them in with the adults, and last week, when Mrs. Barrington died, young Ginger Farning got a nasty fright."

Ruth's eyes had lit up with a quick interest. "Martin was telling me something about your idea for a new wing – but I mustn't keep you talking. Ilena wants to get home to her bed." Ruth pressed his arm. "Try to manage dinner with us when you're less busy. I want to hear about this children's wing of yours – and do please insist that Ilena keeps her appointment at my consulting-rooms tomorrow. She'll probably want to go rushing off to a hat show, but she'll do herself more harm than good if she doesn't have that iron deficiency of hers put right."

They said good-bye, then he accompanied Ilena home to Routledge Court.

"Go and jump into bed," he ordered, when they entered the flat. "I'll brew some coffee and nursemaid you for half an hour."

When he carried the tray into Ilena's bedroom, she was look-

144

ing exquisitely fragile in her big bed, clad in a lacy bed-jacket with a mound of silk pillows piled up behind her.

"Here we are." Paul put the tray on the bed between them and filled the two cups. Ilena smiled at him as she took her cup and saucer. "You are going to make a nice husband, Paul," she said.

"Good." He sipped his coffee and watched her with professional eyes rather than lover-like ones. "You're looking a bit more rested now," he decided.

"It was so silly of me to faint."

"Ruth said you're seeing her at her consulting-rooms to-morrow."

"No, I don't think it is necessary –"

"Now don't be obstinate, Ilena. Ruth thinks you need a check-up, and she's too busy a person to play about – and you've got to admit you've been very on edge lately."

"I – I suppose so." She put down her cup and saucer and nervously fingered the big diamond on her left hand. "It has been all these preparations for the wedding, they have tired me. And then, too, you have been much concerned with your work – I sometimes think you care more about it than you care for me."

"Naturally my work's important to me." He regarded her with a sudden frown. "You've always known that, but once I've operated on little Ginger –"

"Ginger, Ginger!" She moved sharply, jarring the coffee tray. "I am growing tired of the name! Always your patients have to intrude into our personal life, and it isn't fair to me. You put the Clinic before me, and it isn't fair."

"Ilena, you're getting yourself worked up –"

"I have reason! You talk of being treated with indifference, but does it ever occur to you that I resent taking second place to a stone building and a lot of misplaced bones?" Her resentful eyes swept his face. "When you have operated on this child will you *try* to spare a little time for me?"

"Sure, Ilena." He broke into a smile and patted her hand. "All the arrangements for the operation are made, you know. I'm having the anaesthetist from the Stepney Memorial, and the boy himself is prepared now to face the operation on Wednesday. He hasn't a naturally robust constitution, and it's been Marny's splendid help which has made it possible for me to get him into a good enough physical and mental shape to undergo major surgery."

Marny!

The name jarred through Ilena and she went taut against her silk pillows.

"*Mon dieu*," she exclaimed, "if I am not hearing about the crippled child, then I am hearing about that indispensable secretary of yours! Secretaries usually are indispensable when they are violently in love with their employers," she added waspishly.

"Good God, the things you say, Ilena!" He stood up, flushing like a boy. "Marny, as I told you earlier on, is marrying my radiographer."

"And you do not like it, do you, Paul?"

"Stow it!" He leant over Ilena and gave her an angry shake. "I'm not going to argue with you tonight, least of all about Marny." Then he straightened to his full height, blocking the flow of light from the bedside lamp so that Ilena seemed to lie in his shadow. Her hair was dark against her pillows; tiny shadows deepened the unusual blue of her eyes, and Paul could see the lift and fall of her shapely breasts beneath the lace of her bedjacket.

"I don't know why we're always arguing about Marny," he
146

said, rather wearily. "You know full well that if I wanted to play around I wouldn't do so with a mere child."

"Oh, you men and all your noble talk!" Ilena's face suddenly held the age-old anger of all women, who would cast out men if their bodies would only let them. "To all of you a woman is no more than a means of expressing your own self-love and self-esteem. A cock as it crows on a barn door is more honest than the lot of you. He at least crows openly and not behind closed doors."

"Am I the specific target, Ilena, for all this philosophising on the meretricious nature of the male of the human species?" Paul gazed down at her, quizzically. "Looking back over our courtship I realize that I haven't always put you before my work, but I warned you when we got engaged that if you took me, you took the Clinic as well. But I deny your implication that all men want women for the same reason. I want one because I want companionship and love. Love, Ilena, not just passion. That's a fairly cheap commodity and on sale to any man with a fiver in his wallet. Love is something else . . . a man gets hungry for it in a way that's even beyond the understanding of some of you women, and it's said, I know, that women are the greater lovers because they are also mothers . . ."

"You want to be mothered?" she murmured.

"No, but I do want to be loved." He bent and brushed his lips across her forehead. "Get some sleep, you need it. And don't forget to go and see Ruth in the morning."

"Paul —" her hand clutched his overcoat sleeve; her eyes were wild and fatigue-smudged in her lovely white face, "don't go away angry."

"Now come on, relax," he murmured. "You'll never sleep, all tensed up like this."

"I want a sleeping pill."

"Those darn things!" But he saw she wouldn't sleep until he let her take one, so he strode to the bathroom for a little cold water, and when he returned she was sitting up and shaking about a dozen of the tiny glistening pills into the palm of her hand. She watched, under her jetty lashes, the look that came on his face.

"Ilena, give me that bottle, and the pills in your hand!" He forcibly took them from her; his nostrils showed chalk-white, while a picture of Nadia's slashed wrists sprang vividly into his mind in that moment.

Tuesday wasn't a comfortable day at the Clinic. Paul didn't need Marny in the office, so during the morning she helped out in the gym. It rained in the afternoon and she and Ginger played marbles on his bedroom floor until it was time for his nap. Then she made her way downstairs, for Paul sometimes had one or two letters which he wanted to get in the post before five o'clock.

Errol was in the hall talking to a nurse, from whom he excused himself when Marny passed him. He caught up with her at the door of the office. "Darlin', I want to see you after work this evening," he said. "I've something to show you."

"All right — only leave me alone now, Errol, please!" She tried to pull away from him, but he held her a moment longer and regarded her with wanting, tawny eyes. They were standing like that, in the attitude of an embrace, when Paul suddenly came out of the dispensary across the hall and saw them. Marny at once wrenched free of Errol and hurried into the office. She heard him exchange a few words with her employer, then she turned blindly to the filing cabinet and was pretending to sort through some folders when Paul walked into the office. She hoped he'd go straight through to his sitting-room, but his desk chair scraped the floor and he sat down.

"I've a letter I want to get off before five o'clock," he said curtly. "Perhaps you could mess about with those folders afterwards."

She flushed and came to his desk. She sat down and flipped open her shorthand pad. Paul proceeded to dictate his letter, his grey eyes fixed inscrutably upon the fireplace beyond her bent head. He had almost finished dictating when there was a tap on the door and a girl from the kitchen brought in their afternoon tea.

"Take mine through to the sitting-room, Ivy," Paul said. "I'll have it in there."

"Yes, Mr. Stillman." The girl put Marny's cup down on the desk, then she carried the tray with the remaining cup into the adjacent sitting-room. After she had gone, Paul went in to drink his tea alone, shutting the door on Marny.

She stirred her tea, lifted the cup and – splash – a big teardrop dimpled it. The cup rattled in the saucer as she put it down and hurriedly dragged a handkerchief from her sleeve. She mopped at her eyes, blinking fiercely to try and stem the silly tears, for she felt she would die of humiliation if Paul walked back into the office and caught her crying.

But he didn't come back, and by the time she had typed his letter she was restored to a measure of calmness and her eyelids were not quite so pink.

It was almost five o'clock. Marny waited another five minutes for Paul to come back, then in the end she reluctantly tapped upon the connecting door. She couldn't post his letter until he had signed it.

"Come in." His voice was lazy, uninterested, and when Marny walked into his sitting-room she found him sprawled on the long couch, blowing smoke rings at the ceiling.

"Will you please sign this, Mr. Stillman." She held out the

letter. "You said you wanted to get it into the post before five."

"Oh – sure." He swung his long legs to the floor and took the letter from her hand. The action was carelessly quick on his part and the glowing tip of the cigarette in his fingers brushed against Marny's thumb, searing the cushion of flesh just below it.

She carried the thumb quickly to her mouth, while tears of pain stung her eyelids.

"Gee, I'm sorry, Marny!" Paul flicked the offending cigarette into an ashtray and the next moment he was standing over her, holding her hand and examining the tiny burn. The skin wasn't broken, but he insisted on applying a small dressing. "I'm a careless brute," he murmured. "There, has it stopped stinging?"

"It really isn't anything. I'm sure I'll live."

Her green eyes lifted to his dark face, then he grated: "Damn it, Marny, let's be friends again. I've come to depend so on your friendship."

"No." She shook her red head almost fiercely. "I'm leaving right after Ginger's undergone his operation."

"What?"

"I think you heard me."

"Yes, I heard you." He caught at her with hands that were none too gentle. "What's the matter, you little prude, are you scared I might break loose again and use you for another session of sublimation?"

His words, his eyes cut into her, but she gallantly fought with him. "You were welcome to the sublimation, for what it was worth," she retorted, "but it was really rather cruel of you to confess your lapse to Ilena. You must have known she'd warn me off, in case, in my country girl innocence, I had let

150

your sophistication go to my head. As it happens," defiantly, "I haven't."

"You really believe I told Ilena I kissed you?" He almost spluttered the words in his indignation.

"Didn't you?"

"Good lord, no! What do you take me for"

Marny's bottom lip started to tremble, but she determinedly schooled it with her small teeth. "I thought you had told her. She seemed to know, a-and I felt ashamed, betrayed, as though I'd done something dirty."

"My dear girl –"

"Anyway, it doesn't alter anything, that you didn't tell her." Marny pulled free of his hands. "I'm still going away. Now you'd better sign your letter, Mr. Stillman, though it's too late now for the five o'clock post."

His face was an inscrutable mask as he retrieved the letter from the floor and slashed his signature across the bottom of it. "You needn't post it tonight," he said.

"I'm going out," she replied. "I – I have a date with Errol."

"Then take it, by all means." Their eyes clashed, grey ice bearing down on green hostility ... Marny grabbed the letter and fled.

It was still drizzling with rain; large crystal drops spangled the yellowing leaves of the hedges, while the wet grass in the park emitted a poignant, earthy scent. Marny breathed it, and a sudden homesickness for Norfolk clutched at her throat. She ached for familiar things, even for one of Uncle Richard's lectures, and especially for Aunt Marjorie's good-natured face, creased by perplexity as she tried to decide whether she had been wise to let the Vicar's sister manage the boutique stall and whether or not the Ladies' Guild had baked enough cakes for the Scouts' concert. ....

Marny shot Paul's letter into the mouth of the letter-box, and when she turned round she saw Errol's scarlet car tearing down the road towards her. He braked, flung open the door, and she climbed in beside him. "Let's go to the Clairmont in Baker Street," he said.

But before they shot away again he opened the glove compartment of the car and tossed a silk scarf into Marny's lap. "Cover your hair, you're getting soaked," he suggested.

She obediently adjusted the scarf over her hair . . . and breathed the delicate, expensive perfume which clung to the silk.

Unmistakably the perfume which Ilena Justine always used! Marny would have known it anywhere. She stared ahead of her as the scarlet car thrust through the dusk and the drizzle, and it was as though she had always known about Ilena and Errol. There was no real surprise in her, only a raw sort of sadness.

Later on in the evening the Clairmont would be filled with young couples, for it was a bright, modern place with corn-coloured woodwork, contemporary paintings on the walls, and a large record-player. Right now the lounge was almost deserted, though men lolled at the counter of the saloon bar.

Errol ordered drinks while Marny settled herself in a tangerine-coloured armchair. "Thank you," she took her drink from Errol, not quite meeting his eyes as he sat down in a chair facing her. She was painfully sure that he had brought her here to show her a ring.

He studied her, the tremulous flutter of her lashes, the absence of colour in her cheeks. She had removed the silk scarf and her hair clung in damp, glistening tendrils above her eyes. She looked so young . . . and yet not quite so young as she had been.

"I said I had something to show you. Be feminine and curious and ask what it is," he coaxed.

She tried gallantly to meet his eager mood, forcing back the tide of unhappiness which kept threatening to engulf her. "What is it, Errol?"

"As though I didn't know!" she thought wildly.

He grinned, then took a small, heart-shaped jeweller's box out of a pocket of his driving coat. He opened the little box. The pink pearl glowed soft and lovely on a bed of tiny diamonds, whose fiery sparks enclosed the pearl, burning about it with the desire that was in Errol's eyes.

She felt him take hold of her left hand, then the ring was glistening on her third finger. "Now you're mine!" he exulted. "Now you're my girl, Marny."

The following day Ginger underwent his operation and for several days afterwards he was in the exclusive care of nurses.

Marny missed being with him, and it wasn't until Saturday morning that Paul took her up to the boy's room for a short visit. The operation had plainly drained his strength for a while, but Paul was proud of the job he had done, and he assured Marny, when they left Ginger's room, that the boy would soon be sitting up again and taking notice.

They walked along the corridor towards the stairs. Their hands unexpectedly brushed, and Marny's heart fluttered in her throat when Paul's slender fingers touched the ring she wore. Then he said, almost casually: "When do you want to leave me?"

"I'd like to go as soon as possible," she replied. "You shouldn't have any trouble getting another secretary. I'll get in touch with an agency and see about it for you, if you like."

"Efficient to the last," he drawled.

"I don't want to leave you stranded." They had now reached the foot of the stairs. Marny could hear the phone ringing in the office and she hurried to answer it. Ruth Stein was on the line, asking for Paul. Marny handed him the receiver, then she carried his coffee tray to the kitchen, and upon her return to the office she was unexpectedly told by Paul that the Steins, who had recently moved into a new house, were throwing a house-warming party the following evening and Ruth had suggested that Marny might like to bring her fiancée.

"Are you going?" The question escaped from Marny before she could stop it.

Paul looked quizzical. "Do you mind? Ruth and her husband are old friends of mine." Then hearing footsteps he glanced round towards the half-open door. Errol strolled into the room, carrying some X-ray pictures in his hand. "You wanted to see these," he said.

Paul was smiling in a way Marny didn't like. "The Steins are having a house-warming tomorrow evening, Dennis," he said. "You and Marny are invited."

Errol's mobile eyebrows flickered comically and Marny felt certain he was going to turn the invitation down flat. Then to her dismay he accepted the invitation with rather ironical alacrity.

The following evening Marny prepared for the Steins' party in an extremely tense frame of mind. In an attempt to relieve her own tension she slipped into one of her favourite outfits, a delicate pastel green and pink chiffon kaftan. She arranged her hair very simply, and a tiny silver-strung heart glittered in the youthful hollow of her throat.

She met her own eyes in the mirror of the dressing-table, and the look in them was rather appalling. She looked desperate about something . . . like a creature trapped in a corner.

154

She snatched her fur jacket off the bed and hurried from the bungalow.

The majority of the Steins' guests were medical people, but Ruth and her husband were both of a lively turn of mind, so they had a lively circle of medical friends. Ilena and Paul were obviously acquainted with everyone present, and it was a relief to Marny that her employer hardly seemed to notice her presence. Ilena looked fabulous in coffee lace, with the back of her gown plunging in a V to her waist. When she saw Marny she actually deigned to smile, then her petrol-blue glance slipped deliberately to Errol, and Marny felt herself plunge down into a private hell of resentment.

Ruth approached Marny a little later in the evening and asked her to play the piano. "I know from Paul that you play. Extremely well, he tells me."

The request embarrassed Marny, but it would have been ungracious to say no to Ruth. Her green eyes flashed across the room to where Paul was standing, they signalled a reproof which his mouth mocked, then he lifted his cigar in that arrogant way of his and she was sure he used it to hide a rather nasty smile.

Marny always played well when she was emotionally disturbed, and those among the guests who expected pretty-pretty music from this slender thing in the apple-blossom gown were startled and delighted by her assured touch on the piano keys and the individuality which she brought to the Chopin pieces she played.

She escaped into the party crowd when she eventually rose from the baby grand, and feeling rather flushed and warm she sought a little coolness in a rather pretty conservatory adjacent to the drawing-room. A fountain tinkled into a goldfish pool, and Marny sat down on a seat that was screened by a small

155

plantation of indoor plants. They threw their shadow over her, and for several minutes she felt peacefully isolated from everyone ... then her back stiffened at the sudden approach of footsteps. Two pairs, one masculine, the other undoubtedly belonging to a woman. The couple paused, and Marny instinctively drew back into the screening plants.

"Look, this is a bit risky," Marny heard the man say, and right away she recognized the voice ... lilting, Irish, unmistakable.

"But you like taking risks, you wicked wretch. Or so you have always said." Those seductive, accented tones were also unmistakable, and for a wild moment Marny trembled on the verge of revealing herself. She didn't want to overhear a clandestine conversation between Paul's fiancée and her own. She didn't want to sit here and undergo the torment of this.

Then Errol spoke again. "We broke things off that last time you came back from Paris," he said. "We agreed then that our affair had lost its savour, and seeing you tonight hasn't changed my mind, Ilena, if you were hoping it had."

"*Mon dieu*, you are the most conceited creature I have ever known! Do you think I cannot live without your peasant's arms around me?"

"I don't think you can live long without a man," he retorted. He laughed, there was a sudden scuffle, then a small, sharp exclamation of pain from Errol. "You damn tigress, you almost had my eye out with those scarlet daggers – you've drawn blood! Look!"

"Errol ... *chéri* ... here is my handkerchief!"

"You go to the devil! I'm going back to the drawing-room among civilized people!"

His footsteps retreated. Ilena didn't move for about a minute; Marny could just see her through the fronds of the screen-

156

ing plants. She was staring blindly in front of her, curiously stricken, curiously lost, so that Marny had to pity her.

Spoilt, self-indulgent, a victim of her own tempestuous impulses.

Yes, Marny had to pity her, but she didn't relax in her seat until Ilena had gone back into the house. Then Marny realized that where before she had been warm, she was now quite cold. She shivered and wrapped her slim, bare arms about her own body. She wasn't aware for a moment or two that her nostrils had tensed to the aromatic drift of cigar smoke.

She slowly, almost fearfully turned her head ... and her green eyes locked with the grey eyes of her employer.

"You!"

He might have been graven in stone, then his cigar butt described an arc to the tiled floor of the conservatory, and Marny was held motionless, transfixed on the silver rapiers that were his eyes. Then he moved, found her with his hands, and she cried out as he lifted her.

"Shut up!" His hands tumbled her hair. "Be quiet!"

"No –"

"Be quiet!"

He gathered her savagely against him, and there in the fragrant dimness of the conservatory, where a fountain tinkled like faint bells, Paul kissed Marny as she had never dreamed of being kissed, until it seemed that her breath would stop, her heart break, the world shatter.

And she clung to him, knowing now that she had wanted this with every fibre from the first moment she had seen him. On Knighton Sands with the muscles running smoothly under his bare skin. In the dawn light, with grief in his heart. Now, when anger burned like a flame in him.

"Oh – Paul!"

His name broke from her as their lips broke apart.

"Oh – you!" he groaned. "If you hadn't been here, I'd have broken that lovely, lying neck of Ilena's."

She lay in the hard, warm prison of his arms, and there was love throughout her body for this man. There was no part of her that belonged to herself any more; he had taken everything. Her lashes tumbled as she felt his lips again, touching her face, her mouth, her throat . . .

Then he had suddenly put her away from him. He raked the tousled hair back from his eyes. "Go back to the party," he grated. "Go on, scat! I'm not good company right now."

But she didn't move. She was poignant with the desire to hold him and ease him. He saw this. The compassion in her eyes . . . the mother wish to kiss the hurt and make it better.

"Oh, get out!" he snapped. "Don't you know when you're not wanted?"

She fled then, her tiny silver slippers tapping the tiles, her apple-blossom dress frothing, a bruise stinging her bottom lip.

She found Errol. "I want to go home," she said. He didn't argue with her; perhaps he, too, was glad to get away from the party.

They drove silently through the night, and Marny knew that she had failed dismally in her effort to secure Paul's happiness. She had never loved or wanted Errol; she had only hoped to keep him away from the girl whom Paul loved.

CHAPTER IX

A HAND shook Marny out of troubled sleep. "Marny," Nurse Truscott was bending over her in the glow of the bedside lamp, "Mr. Stillman sent me over for you. Ginger isn't any too well. He keeps asking for you."

"Ginger?" Marny sat up sharply.

The next moment she had thrust back the bedcovers and was scrambling into her dressing-gown and slippers. Together she and Scotty hurried across the night-wrapped Clinic grounds, and a few minutes later they were entering the room in which Ginger lay.

Paul turned from the bedside, and noticing Marny's white, frightened face he at once stepped across to her. "I'm sorry to drag you out of bed," he said. "The boy has developed a rather high temperature and he keeps saying your name. I think he'll sleep if you'll sit with him for a while."

"Of course I'll sit with him." She brushed past Paul and went to the bed. Ginger broke into a faint smile when he saw her.

"Hullo, darling." She sat down beside him and took his small hot hand into hers. "Now why aren't you fast asleep like a good boy?"

"I wanted you," he said fretfully. "I thought you'd gone away."

"I've only been to a party," she assured him gently.

"Was it – was it a nice party?" His hot little fingers curled about hers.

"Oh, very splendid," she said. "We had lots of nice things

to eat and all the guests were dressed in their very best clothes."

"Did you all dance and sing?"

"We did a little of each, darling, you know how it is at a party." And as Marny said that, she felt the restless shifting of Paul's tall figure, for he stood just beyond the muted glow of the lamp on the bedside cabinet, one hand clenched a little against the side of his dark evening trousers.

He had not yet been to bed, Marny realized.

"Sing now, Marny," Ginger pleaded. "Sing about the lily and the man."

A faint, sweet pink crept into her cheeks, then very gently she sang the Tennyson song which so appealed to this child, whose imagination she had awoken with her own love of the beautiful and the fey. He drifted off to sleep before the song ended, but Marny sang it through to the end:

> "Now folds the lily all her sweetness up,
> And slips into the bosom of the lake;
> So fold thyself, my dearest, thou, and slip
> Into my bosom and be lost in me."

She sat quietly, her head a little bent, until Paul drew her to her feet.

"He's sleeping, now you must sleep," Paul said.

She felt the gentleness of his hands and her legs weakened dangerously at his proximity. She must have lost her colour again, for he added gruffly: "I'd better give you a tot of brandy before you go back to the bungalow."

"I – I'm all right –"

"You look like a small ghost." He turned to Nurse Trus-cott, who stood regarding the pair of them with friendly but inquisitive eyes. "Keep an eye on the boy, Scotty. I'll be up again in a short while."

"Right you are, Paul."

Marny felt his arm along her back as they made their way downstairs, and the words of the song she had sung to Ginger were going round and round in her mind. My dearest, thou! My dearest – She hadn't dared to face the full truth of that until tonight, and now she was overwhelmed by her feeling for Paul.

They reached the hall and Marny slipped free of his arm. She turned to say she was going straight to the bungalow, but her words died before they were born. Paul looked as ravaged as she by a war of inner emotions, and silently she preceded him into the office. They walked through to his sitting-room, where he switched on the electric fire and poured brandy into a couple of balloon glasses. Marny took hers and sat down on a leather pouffe near the fire. She gazed into her brandy glass as though it were a crystal ball.

"What do you see?" Paul murmured.

"Only a swirl of vapour, nothing tangible."

"That isn't quite the truth, is it – my dearest?"

She lifted wild green eyes to his face. Then she jumped to her feet, set aside her brandy glass and went running past him to the door.

She didn't make it. He swooped and caught her.

"Sweetheart – my baby!" His voice shook, and she wildly fought his arms as she felt the touch of them. She had to fight to resist them. She knew it was essential she fight to resist them. She knew it was essential she fight because she wanted them so much – too much –

"No, Paul – please!" she entreated, and her sudden tears were on his face as he held her close and carried her to the couch that faced the fireplace.

"Stop fighting me," he ordered as he sat down with her. "This isn't sublimation, you sweet fool. It never was, I know that now." His hand caressed her hair. "My little love – warm – real – throughout every sweet morsel that composes you."

Her strength, her will-power ebbed away like sea-wrack on the tide, and suddenly she and Paul were kissing, without thinking. They didn't want to think. They clung closely, fearful of all the outside things that could force them apart. She heard his turbulent, boyish, whispered endearments; thrilling her blood, even shocking her a little, but wanted so much. Gathered in by her at last, a waiting harvest that had somehow grown richer for the waiting.

They had both been waiting, for she felt now how starved for real affection was this big, warm, compassionate man who gave so much of himself to other people. She felt him tremble when she wrapped her arms around him and touched him with her lips.

"I love you, Paul." Her words melted against his throat. "I love you." And it was an inexpressible peace for both of them that she had said it at last and he had heard her say it.

In a while they grew calmer, until they were just sitting quietly with their arms about one another.

"How I've hated the last few days, that wretched coldness between us," he said. Then he gave her a reproving shake. "How dare you think I'd tell anyone, least of all Ilena, that you ever let me lose myself in your arms!"

"I'm sorry," she whispered.

"And so you should be."

He brushed her tip-tilted nose with his lips, but now he had said Ilena's name. Now the magic was dying and Marny was pressing his arms away from her. At once he gathered her savagely close to him, hurting her a little. "I can't let you go, Marny." He spoke in a raw, hard, very male voice. "Not yet – not just yet. I've only just discovered you, and if I let you go too quickly I shall tear open inside."

She felt his lips against her temple. "My dear, how was I to know the world could hold someone like you? A man dreams of someone like you, when he's a boy, but the years go by, the yearning piles up, so that an inevitable headlong infatuation for someone is bound to occur."

Their eyes met. Ilena stood between them, as they had last seen her . . . curiously stricken . . . curiously lost.

"I – I feel trapped," Paul groaned.

"Darling –"

"I don't love her. You don't love Errol Dennis. What the hell were you up to, offering yourself like some sacrifice to – to that damn young pagan!"

A sacrifice to a pagan god! Marny half smiled and pressed her hands against the firm, warm nape of Paul's neck. Her hands adored him. He was so – so good to touch, and his skin had a fresh, scrubbed smell overlaid by a wisp of cigars and the tang of coal-tar soap.

He felt her hands wandering down over the hard bones of his shoulders, and a fluid tenderness that was also an anguish gripped him. He wanted to think straight, to sort out their problem, but her dressing-gown had opened enough to show him the slim white column of her neck, the ruffle of pink nylon that lifted and fell with her breathing. Thinking gave way to feeling, and Marny heard him whisper her name in a new way. She also felt his quickened breathing, and her heart flipped, half frightened as she realized what she was doing to him, sitting half undressed in his lap.

She pulled out of his arms and stood away from him. He

watched her with knowing, quizzical, slightly frustrated eyes, above which his dark hair was tousled from her hands.

"You scared little puss," he mocked, but she saw that his mouth was indulgent with love.

"W – we've got to be sensible." She walked to the fireplace, where she stood gazing at the Van Gogh, painting, "Don't you remember what you said, Paul, about the life-giving element in passion being important? It is important. Far more important than giving in to our feelings, and cheapening our love."

"You're damnably right, of course," he growled, "but I'm not particularly consoled."

She turned to look at him and saw the grim smile curling the edges of his mouth.

"Our love," he repeated. "It's like saying our child or our house, but we're never going to have a child together or live in a house together – we both know it."

His face then was darkly bitter, and Marny fled to him and knelt down on the floor, her face buried against his knees. He stroked her hair, running his slender, sensitive fingers through its softness. "I can't let Ilena down," he said. "I daren't. You saw her face tonight – you know as well as I that she wouldn't hesitate to do herself some sort of harm."

Marny knew he was thinking of Nadia and she trembled, there against his knees. "You wouldn't be you, Paul, and I wouldn't love you the way I do if you could turn your back on someone in need," she whispered. "And I'm going away, so that should make things a little easier for you."

She felt his hand grow still on her hair.

"I must go, Paul," she insisted, "for our sakes and Ilena's."

"It is the only way, of course," he at last agreed in a sombre voice. Then with sudden passion he gathered her back into his arms and for one moment more she allowed herself the heavenly luxury of being held by him. She felt his lips against her lashes, felt them touch the tip of her nose, then she was held in a sweet helplessness, a little murmur breaking from her as his firm, demanding lips sought the ultimate of response from hers. There was love, savagery and hopelessness in his kiss, and all this Marny answered before she left him and returned to the bungalow.

Ginger's condition grew no worse after his flare-up of temperature Sunday night. Marny, however, remained anxious about him. Somehow he sensed her imminent departure and for several days she postponed her going for the child's sake.

She and Paul worked constrainedly together, avoiding all intimate conversation, shrinking from physical contacts, finding out that love is intolerable when it cannot be expressed.

It was on the Wednesday afternoon that things reached a state of climax between them. Marny was coming out of Ginger's room, laughing a little because he had wanted to know why he always looked upside down in a spoon, and she walked straight into Paul in the corridor.

Raw longing made his eyes blaze silver as for a moment they brushed against one another. Then they stood apart, tensed as a pair of caged creatures.

"Ginger is heaps better," she said shakily.

He knew what she meant, and she heard the drag of his breath.

"I wish I could die rather than leave you, Paul," she whispered.

"Where will you go, Marny? Home to Norfolk?"

"No, I don't think I want to go home."

"But, darling," his look turned to one of quick anxiety,

"I took it for granted you'd go home."

"I may get another job, Paul. Then again I may enrol at the London School of Music and take on a flat. I have an allowance, you know, from the money my mother left me. I – I don't depend on a wage."

"I can't bear to think of you all alone." His eyes dwelt with hunger on her pale young face. "Oh, God, I'd like to chuck everything and just go off with you. Why should we sacrifice ourselves in this way?"

"Because I value your honour, my dear," she replied. "And also because your work is important to you and I would never ask you to throw it all up. You've striven to build your Clinic into a place that's become of real benefit to people, and much as I love and need you, my need must take second place to that of the people who come to you to be eased of their pain . . ."

Then she broke off as Alec Gordon came hurrying round a corner towards them.

"Ah, I wanted you, Mr. Stillman!" He paused for a few words with Paul about a patient, and Marny quickly noticed the abstraction of Paul's replies, the effort it was for him to pay attention to what his assistant was saying.

"Will you come with me now and take a look at Mr. Holroyd?" Alec was urging him. "I'm worried about the old chap, and that's a fact."

"Not right now – later." Paul was looking at Marny. She saw the spreading hunger in his eyes, the desire to be with her to the exclusion of everything else, even his duty to his patients, and she knew he was entirely in her hands in this moment, like a piece of putty she could shape or destroy.

"Please go with Alec," she said. "We can talk later."

"Please, please go with him!" her green eyes implored. "Don't be destroyed by mere desire for me. Don't, please, let

166

us turn our love into something we shall both end by hating."

Then, before he could say anything, she walked away. Paul watched her go. He knew she was giving him back to his work and he tried to be grateful. But, dammit, he wasn't! He was fiercely resentful of everything that was keeping them apart, and it was all he could do not to plunge after her, to snatch her in his arms and let love destroy the pair of them.

He became aware that Alec Gordon was regarding him with a puzzled frown.

"Let's go and see Holroyd," he said.

Paul didn't find out until a couple of hours later that Marny had left the Clinic. He found her good-bye note on the mantelpiece in his sitting-room. She had written:

Dear Paul,

Forgive me for running away, but I love you too much to stay. Later on it may be possible for us to meet as friends again. I hope so with all my heart, for I should not like to lose complete touch with you and Ginger, and the friends I have made at the Clinic. Please return Errol's ring for me. I somehow think he will accept it without surprise and with more sweet grace than I believe you think him capable of. If things had been different, if I had wanted less from love than it's in my nature to want, then I might have married Errol.

Paul, please don't worry about me. Worry only about your work, and be as sweet to Ilena as you have always been to me.

Later, when the pain of her going had turned to a dull ache, he wandered about the office, which seemed colourless and desolate without Marny in it. Even on a dull day her bright hair had brought sunshine into the room. He opened the drawers of her desk and touched the pencils, the envelopes, the things she had touched. There was a forgotten lipstick in one of the drawers, and he held the little gilt tube in his hand, his fingers clenching on it as he seemed to feel her lips beneath his again. Soft, sweet, a little shy until desire flamed through her slim body. . . .

The lipstick clattered sharply back into the drawer. Paul slammed the drawer and strode back into his sitting-room.

His housekeeper awaited him. She wanted to know what sweet he fancied with his dinner that evening, and he stared at her as though she were talking to him in Chinese.

"Aren't you feeling well, Mr. Stillman?" she asked, noticing with concern his drawn look.

"I've a slight headache — and don't bother about cooking me a dinner, Mrs. Piper. I've decided to go out."

He didn't know where the devil he was going, but he felt he just had to get away from the Clinic for a few hours. Mrs. Piper left him and he took a shower, put on a lounge suit and walked out to his car.

He drove aimlessly, out towards the country. The evening air blew through the open window beside him, cooling his aching temples. The air was slightly moist and earthy and he realized that autumn had come. Autumn, the time of falling leaves and the end of summer. He heard the cawing of crows across the dim, hazy fields and straggling brambles touched the sides of the car when he turned off it the main road. He had recognized that he was near the Surrey Windmill and he decided on impulse to have a meal there.

It was a picturesque place, with black and white timbers and a thatched roof. As Paul swung the car into the parking lot, he heard the splash of the ancient mill-wheel that was still kept turning for the pleasure of the people who came to dine in the riverside garden. Paul, however, had no wish this evening to dine under the stars and the trees, where he might hear the fluting of a blackbird and breathe the scent of the big double tea-roses that were a speciality of the Surrey Windmill.

He picked at his dinner in the oak panelled dining-room, and afterwards he went into the bar, where he ordered a rum and lemon. There were several in the bar and he drifted into conversation with a local resident.

The place, the couple of drinks he had, his conversation with a pleasant stranger, were narcotics, dulling pain and thought; shutting out for a while his bleak awareness that when he returned to the Clinic, Marny would no longer be there.

During the next few days there was a certain amount of subdued speculation at the Clinic concerning Marny's abrupt departure.

Nurse Donkin came dangerously close to guessing the truth when she said to Scotty: "I always thought she was a bit too thick with the boss. Perhaps the Imperial Princess turned ratty and Marny decided to get out before there was trouble."

"I hope you aren't suggesting what I think you are?" Scotty's loyalty to Paul was immediately ruffled.

"Oh, come down off your high horse, Scotty," the other nurse said. "You know as well as the rest of us that before his engagement the boss had a quick eye for a nice piece of skirt. Marny Lester was awfully attractive. There was a warmth about her – I liked her a lot. She cheered this place up no end with our little sing-song sessions round the piano. They made a change from the stuff on that blinking television set."

Scotty, who knew Paul very well, had long entertained a

suspicion of his regard for his young secretary, but she had no intention of gossiping about him with her colleagues.

She changed the subject. "I don't mind some of the old films they show on television," she said. "I saw an awful good one a few weeks back."

She and Nurse Donkin drifted into film talk, and Marny receded to the back of their minds. They would miss her, for they had both liked her, but she wouldn't haunt them as she haunted Paul.

He fought his battle with comparative success while he was working, but the nights tormented him, for then he was alone with his thoughts. He couldn't sleep, and he spent hours sitting up in bed, going over his patients' case histories and smoking. Mrs. Piper soon began to find burn holes in his sheets, and when she mentioned the fact he snapped at her not to pester him with her household problems. If she didn't like mending the sheets, then she was at liberty to buy some new ones!

"It isn't that, sir," she objected. "I'm frightened you might fall off to sleep and catch the bed alight."

"I shan't, Mrs. Piper," he assured her grimly. "I wish to hell I could sleep."

Mrs. Piper decided that he was suffering from nerves owing to his rapidly approaching wedding. With motherly concern for him she began to dose him with Horlicks last thing at night, and he sardonically permitted her to do so.

He packed his days and his evenings with work, and knew a fleeting relief spiced with bitterness when Ilena went over to Paris for her final trousseau fittings.

So far the secretarial agency had sent him two shorthand-typists and he had managed to upset both of them. The first had been grubby, and he had a distinct aversion to grubby females. The second had never learnt how to spell. The continual sight of her rubbing out misspelt words had been too much for his nerves in their present ragged state, and he had sent her packing after two days.

He sometimes felt that he was going quietly crazy.

It was perhaps inevitable that Errol Dennis should think Marny had fled to get away from him. He said as much to Paul one morning. "I rushed the kid," he said. "I knew she didn't care as much for me as I cared for her, but I wanted her and I played on her sympathy. I had no right to do that. I forced her into a position from which she had to bolt – or be chewed up."

"Marny wasn't running away from you, Dennis."

The words were out of Paul's mouth before he could stop them . . . then he and Errol were staring at one another.

"You, Stillman?"

Anger flared in Errol's tawny eyes. A quick, flickering anger like lightning, followed almost at once by the realization that if Marny had grown to care for Paul, then such caring had not been aroused by sessions of clandestine love-making in Paul's office. Errol knew women too well! He had long been skilled in sorting the dross from the gold and until Marny's advent into his rather reckless life he had preferred the dross to the gold.

Errol studied Paul's face and he wondered what was going on behind that hard, impassive mask. Was it Ilena he cared for . . . or Marny? Then Errol told himself it had to be Ilena if Stillman had let Marny go away; the gay Irishman could not conceive of a man being altruistic enough to give up someone he might want with all his heart for the sake of keeping a promise made to another woman. You'd have to be one hell of an altruist to do that!

Curiosity grew in the tawny eyes resting on Paul, who stood

scribbling notes concerning a patient.

"Marny was a pretty wonderful little girl," Errol murmured, watching that rigid profile, holding his breath, wondering if Stillman would give himself away.

"Yes," Paul replied, in a perfectly ordinary voice.

"Heavenly to kiss – wasn't she?" Errol said deliberately.

Paul's breath caught sharply. "Damn you, Dennis!"

"For God's sake, the man she cared for would have to care in return. It would be inevitable as the moon rising each month, the rain rushing down into the warmth of the earth . . . I could go on."

Paul stood controlled and very still, outwardly in command of himself again. But he was unable to control the little nerve that flickered beside his mouth.

"You sublime fool!" Errol wanted to say.

After work that evening Errol entered a telephone box and rang Ilena's flat. He knew she had returned from Paris that day.

"I want to se you," he said, when she came on the line. "Will you come to my place or shall I come over to Routledge Court?"

"We have nothing to talk about," she argued.

"You'd be surprised, *chère amie*," he drawled. "Come to my place."

"You – really want me to?"

"I can't wait to see you." He grinned and put down the receiver.

His flat was in a converted Regency house near the Chelsea Embankment, and he drove straight home tonight, not stopping off at a restaurant for his usual evening meal. He garaged his car and walked past the Embankment to the quiet road where he lived. His flat was on the third floor of the white-painted house and decorated with taste in the Regency style. He had brought some of the pieces over from his run-down home in Ireland, where long ago the wild picturesque Dennises had held their hunt balls and their stag parties and slowly ground down the family fortune into a mere two hundred a year. Errol stood smiling ironically at his Waterford wall-lights, thinking of the many times Ilena had called him an Irish peasant. It had amused him to let her think it. She had always liked playing Queen Catherine to his court jester, but in reality the jest was on her. He was not an Irish peasant, and it occasionally shamed him to remember that he was an Irish gentleman.

He was mixing a drink when the doorbell rang; Ilena had once had a key, but he had made her return it.

He put down the shaker and went to the door. As always Ilena was strikingly turned out. Her suit was a clear mimosa yellow and a black sombrero hat shaded her eyes, which were alluringly made up. Her mouth glowed poppy-red against her white, enticing skin.

"You're looking blooming," Errol complimented her.

She walked into the sitting-room and he followed her noticing all the old, small, exciting details about her. The incredible heels of her shoes, that made her walk so precariously that a man instinctively prepared to catch hold of her, certain that she was going to trip over. Then his glance slipped to the dark sheer stockings she always wore; further to the sensuous curve of her hips. . . .

He switched on the wall-lights, for he had things to say to Ilena, and he didn't intend to be sidetracked by the glamorous sight of her in the muted glow of the couchside lamp.

He poured out their drinks and brought them to the Regency

couch to which she had lowered her elegant figure. "Here's to old times, Ilena," he said, lifting his glass.

"The old times are over," she retorted. "You wanted it that way, remember?"

"I remember many things, Ilena, and I ask myself whether either of us will ever really forget them."

He watched her lashes flicker down over her eyes and the black brim of her hat threw her face into a mysterious stillness. She had the exotic beauty of a white orchid, Errol thought, and his blood was suddenly stirred by the old memories.

"Ilena," he said quietly, "is your conscience so untroubled that you can go through with this marriage of yours?"

"W-what do you mean?" She took a rather defiant sip at her drink.

"Don't you think Stillman's worth rather more than another man's leavings?" he asked brutally.

"Oh – to call me that!" She drew back sharply against the striped satin of the Regency couch.

"Aren't you, *chère amie*?" He leant forward, his eyes flickering over her. "My leavings? What have you left to give Stillman that I haven't already taken?"

"My heart."

"Your heart?" He laughed callously as he walked to the sideboard and poured himself another drink. "You've everything but a heart! Stillman only had to let you down once because he had a patient to attend to, and out of sheer, darned pettishness you encouraged me to flirt with you."

"That isn't true!" she snapped.

But it was. One evening Paul had been unable to take her out owing to a flap at the Clinic, so she had gone to a chemin-de-fer party with some friends. Errol had been there, and Ilena, who had been indulged in her own selfishness from a child;

174

she who had to have her amusements, her pleasures and her toys no matter what, had found Errol Dennis one of the most exciting toys she had ever played with ... exciting for several reasons, his wonderful face, his reckless temperament, and the fact that he was an employee of Paul's. For when Paul put the Clinic first, she hated him.

Her feeling for Paul had always been a strange mixture of hate and love. She had always wanted him on his knees, grovelling and adoring like other men. And yet she had known that he would never grovel, and it was that in him to which she had been drawn.

She had wanted to be mastered by him, in the way of a tigress; she had even wanted to kiss his hands, but each time he turned his attention back to the Clinic she had raged with a kind of primitive panic.

Now she regarded Errol with rather lost eyes. "I love Paul," she said.

"It's a funny kind of love, *chère amie.* In my book love encompasses several emotions to which you are a stranger, like honour, respect and service. You hadn't been engaged to Stillman two months before you were two-timing him with me."

"You – you Irish peasant!" She lifted her Martini glass and threw it straight at Errol. It hit him in the face, where it broke, cutting his cheek. As the sudden bright blood rolled down on to his smoking jacket he imperturbably drew out a handkerchief and held it against the cut.

"I have cut you! I have hurt you!" Ilena kept whispering. Then with sudden frenzy she ran to him. She tried to pull the handkerchief away from his face, but he restrained her with his wiry left hand.

"I have cut your face," she whimpered, rather like a frightened child.

"I've been hurt before this." He released Ilena's wrist and walked into the bathroom, where he thrust his cut cheek beneath the cold water tap. Ilena stood in the doorway watching him.

"You can get me an adhesive plaster out of that cabinet if you like," he said.

She tripped to the cabinet and searched for the tin of plasters. Her hands shook as she opened the tin, and Errol grinned derisively when the lid dropped to the tiled floor. He approached her. "What a damn-fool nurse you'd make," he drawled, taking the piece of plaster from her and watching his face in the cabinet mirror as he covered the cut, which was still bleeding a little.

"Forgive me," she said. "I – I didn't mean to hurt you."

He turned to look at her and saw that her petrol-blue eyes were drowned in tears. He had seen many things in Ilena's eyes, but he had never before seen tears in them. "I'll live," he told her dryly.

Her poppy-red mouth quivered, then she fled into the sitting-room, where she fell weeping across the couch. Errol strolled to her, flicked off her hat and dropped it to a chair. "Now you can weep in comfort," he said, and he sat down in a Regency elbow-chair and calmly lit himself a cigarette. While he smoked he watched her. She trembled as she wept and the skirt of her suit was well above her knees.

She had legs like Dietrich, he thought lazily.

"C-can I have a hanky?" she finally sniffed.

"If you'll promise to stop calling me an Irish peasant," he drawled.

"Why must I not call you one?" She turned a forlorn, smeared face to him.

"Because I'm not, *chérie*." He tossed her a handkerchief.

"Are you so blind that you can't see I'm a throwback like yourself, to the bad old days when our forebears counted their slaves with their gold pieces?" He lifted his cigarette, took a long, hard pull at it. "I guess we deserve one another," he murmured ... and if anyone had called him an altruist in that moment, his handsome face would have turned pretty savage.

Ilena phoned Paul the following morning and asked him to take her to lunch. He said he would meet her in the bar of the Savoy Grill at one o'clock.

When he arrived she saw at once how tired he was looking and she caught at his arm in a new way, the concerned way of friend. "You foolish man, you are working yourself to death!" she scolded him. "Have you not found a new secretary yet?"

"Not yet, Ilena. Shall we have a drink in here?"

"No, let us go in if they have a table. I want to talk to you."

Paul had phoned to reserve a table, and the waiter led them to it. Their meal was brought, and though Ilena ate with appetite, she noticed that Paul barely touched his lunch.

"My poor dear, you are so unhappy, are you not?" she said, and when Paul glanced up he saw the gleam of unexpected tears in Ilena's eyes.

"Paul, will it make you less unhappy if I do this?" She slipped her engagement ring off her finger and placed it on the table. Paul stared at the ring, then at Ilena.

"You are looking at me like a duck in thunder," she smiled.

"Yeah – well –" he thrust a hand through his hair and his grey eyes were confounded. "What am I to think, Ilena? Are you play-acting, or have you taken off the ring for real?"

CHAPTER X

"FOR real, Paul? *Mon dieu*, those uncivilized Canadian expressions of yours!"

"You know what I mean." He touched the ring, which still felt warm from her hand. "Are you breaking our engagement?"

"It is what you want, is it not?"

"Now look here," anger hardened his dark face, where lines etched the sides of his eyes and pain had bitten grooves beside his mouth, "if you're playing with me, Ilena, I'll damn well break that lily-white neck of yours ... as I nearly did a few weeks ago."

Her petrol-blue eyes opened up at that. "*Pardonnez-moi?*"

"I overheard a revealing little conversation between you and Errol Dennis at that house-warming party of Ruth Stein's," Paul grated, his teeth snapping on the words. "I was going to tell you to go to hell, but I'm a medic and obliged to understand certain things about people." His grey eyes took in every detail of the exotic little face confronting him. "I didn't want you doing what Nadia did to herself. There was that incident of the sleeping pills I had to take away from you ..."

He broke off.

She was laughing. Actually laughing. Then her scarlet finger-nails gleamed as she took her tall glass of wine into her hand.

"You are the nicest man in the world, Paul, and I really love you with the better part of myself ... but, *chéri*, I am much too beautiful to die at the tender age of twenty-four."

She lifted her wine glass. Her poppy-red mouth caressed the rim of it. And Paul said a word hardly permissible in polite circles.

"Paul, *chéri*," Ilena looked somewhat hurt by the expression he had just used to describe her, "always there was an ocean of difference between us. Always we knew this, but you knew it to my disadvantage when Marny Lester came into our lives. She talked your language. She was in accord with your sentiments. You could not know, Paul, how your eyes looked when you talked of her. So bright, so eager – so that I could have scratched them out of your head at times."

"You barbaric little throwback!" He broke into a short, reluctant laugh and swallowed his wine, replacing it with a refill.

"Of the cave days, eh, Paul?"

"Undoubtedly. And that kind of thing has its pull. I guess I felt it, for a while." He met her eyes. "Why did you ever agree to marry me, Ilena?"

She half shrugged her elegant shoulders. "You were different from all the other men I had known. You would tame me, I thought, and make a better woman of me. Yes, I actually wanted to be a better woman, and perhaps I might have become one if, one evening, you had not let me down; if I had not gone to a certain chemin-de-fer-party to which Errol had also gone. He is a pagan, that one. He is – oh, he is a wicked wretch!"

She laughed, and yet perhaps inside she cried.

Her glance travelled over Paul's face. "I have hurt you, *mon ami*. Abused your trust in me. Made a mockery of our betrothal. I think I should like to lie down and let you trample me. I – I deserve to be hated by you."

He regarded her with eyes in which there was a tired scorn.

"How does one begin to hate a stranger?" he finally asked her. "I guess that's what you've always been, while Marny – Marny was the sun to your sensuous candlelight. Bright day to your dark night."

After that there was nothing more to be said between them. They rose to leave the Grill, and he picked up the discarded diamond ring and handed it back to her. "Keep it," he said. "If I ever find Marny again I shan't want to give her the blinding dazzle of diamonds."

"Have you no idea where she is, Paul?" Ilena managed to look quite concerned.

"I haven't a clue," he retorted.

When Saturday came Paul drove down to Norfolk to see the Lesters. He hoped they might be able to tell him where Marny was. They were unable to. Her aunt had received several letters from her; each had borne a London postmark, but she had not enclosed her address in any one of them.

"Why did she leave you?" Aunt Marjorie gazed at Paul in bewilderment. "She was so happy working for you. She told me so herself."

Paul flushed slightly, then he explained the circumstances. Richard Lester listened with his hands thrust behind his coat tails, and when Paul finished speaking he said explosively: "Marny was always a thoroughly disruptive female. Let her go, Stillman. Forget her. She'll bring you more trouble than she's worth."

"Richard, what a thing to say!" Aunt Marjorie regarded her husband with shocked eyes.

"Listen, Marjorie, when that girl went to London I knew in my bones that she was going to land herself in some sort of trouble."

"Hardly in trouble, Mr. Lester," Paul protested. "You're

barking up the wrong tree if you think Marny has done anything wrong. She – she's been wonderful in every way."

"Really?" Her uncle looked heavily sarcastic. "You regard it as wonderful for a secretary to encourage her employer to fall besottedly in love with her?"

"That isn't true!" Paul's eyes blazed with anger. "Marny has never encouraged me in any way. She did her level best to keep things strictly impersonal between us. That's why she left the Clinic, and now – now I don't know where the devil she is. I've been in touch with the London School of Music, thinking she might have enrolled as a student, and just about every blasted secretarial agency in London – and outside it."

His grey eyes grew bleak. "She's something I've been looking for all my life, yet now I've lost her, maybe for good. I don't suppose you've the remotest conception what that thought is doing to me inside, and I won't shock your narrow sensibilities by telling you." Paul tuned to Marny's aunt. "Mrs. Lester, if you do get to hear where Marny is, you'll let me know right away, won't you?"

"Of course I will, Mr. Stillman." Aunt Marjorie pressed his arm, genuinely troubled that so worldly and self-possessed a man should look so utterly lost.

It was his eyes! They were a strange, raw silver, like ice that would take just so much pressure, then shatter unexpectedly. They were the eyes of a man passionately in love, and for a moment Marjorie Lester stood on the verge of understanding just how much courage it had taken Marny to run away from him. To run away, when those wonderful grey eyes had probably begged her to stay.

"Mr. Stillman, my niece is bound to tell us where she is before long. She isn't a girl to let us worry indefinitely." Aunt Marjorie gave him a consoling smile. "Now won't you change

181

your mind and stay to dinner? I'm sure my son would like to meet you. He's playing cricket for our local team, you know."

The woman was a kindly soul. Paul quite liked her, but he had to get back to the Clinic.

Thank God he had the Clinic!

That was what he often thought in the weeks that followed, and those weeks brought inevitable changes. Errol Dennis and Ilena were unexpectedly married at Caxton Hall, and afterwards they went off to the south of France. Nadia, grown much stronger now, went to live with her father until the day René Blanchard would be free to come to her.

And Paul, in an effort to quieten his mind, deliberately plunged into a fight with Nell Farning for the custody of Ginger. He wanted the child, and she persistently refused to let Paul adopt him. Paul sought legal aid in the matter and the case got into the newspapers. But if Marny read about the case she didn't mention the fact in any of the fortnightly letters which she wrote to her aunt. Always the envelopes bore a London postmark, but she persistently omitted to include her address.

Paul began to feel that she had gone out of his life for ever; that she had, perhaps, recovered control over her feelings and no longer cared for him.

Then on a dull November morning he sat down at his desk and began to read his mail. His new secretary, a pleasant middle-aged widow who lived close enough to the Clinic not to have to live in, had not yet arrived for work. The office was quiet; there was only the ticking of the clock and the rustle of notepaper in Paul's hands. Tiger was cleaning his paws on a corner of the desk and he lifted an enquiring furry head when his master suddenly caught his breath. Then the cat bristled, perhaps with concern, for the creatures are peculiarly sensitive.

He padded his way across the desk and nuzzled Paul's shoulder, but Paul was intently reading the letter in his hands.

Dear Sir, (it ran)

No doubt you will be surprised to receive a letter from a stranger, but my wife and I are very concerned about the young lady we have working for us.

She worked for you at one time, but we think she had a misunderstanding with her young man, and after that she came to work for us. But we know she isn't any too happy and we would like to see this misunderstanding cleared up. If you know Miss Lester's young man perhaps you would be as good as to tell him that she is working for me, Jake Warner, at the above address.

Miss Marny has no idea I am writing this letter. I think if she knew she would leave us. She is a nice little lass and my wife and I should like to see her happy . . .

Paul turned to the house phone and buzzed Scotty. Directly she came over from the bungalow he explained that he was going to Norfolk for the day and would she tell Alec Gordon, as soon as he showed up, to take charge of things.

Scotty couldn't help noticing the brightness of Paul's eyes, his look of renewed vitality, the elated happiness in his voice.

"Have you found her, Paul?" she asked.

"Yes, I've found her, Scotty!" And in his elation he lifted the plump nurse clear off her feet and swung her round as though she weighed next to nothing. A few minutes later he had left the Clinic and his car was speeding away with all of Errol Dennis's recklessness.

When Paul reached Attleborough he enquired the whereabouts of Jake Warner's farm from the landlord of a pub in the village. The farm turned out to be a fairly extensive place and well tucked away from civilization; the sort of place where a person could probably hide for ever from the outside world, if they so wished.

Ducks and chickens fluttered in the path of the Bentley as Paul drove into the yard that fronted the long, low farmhouse. A woman was hanging clothes to dry on a line at the side of the yard. She turned to look at the car, then came over as Paul climed out from behind the wheel.

"Good day to you!" Her shrewd, countrywoman's eyes took in his smart dark overcoat, the town polish that clung to him. "It's my husband you'll be wantin' to see, no doubt?"

"If your husband's Jake Warner," he agreed. "He wrote me this letter." Paul showed it to her.

"Crikey!" She put a big damp hand against her ample bosom. "Now I was dead against Jake writin' that there letter – 'tis the lass's own business if she don't want nought more to do with her feller."

"Mrs. Warner," Paul's patience had been strained by too many weeks of waiting, longing and hoping, "where can I find her?"

"You – you wouldn't be *him*?" the woman exclaimed.

"I guess I am."

"Deary me! Well, I hope she don't go holdin' this against Jake and me. We're not ones as a rule to go poking our noses where our faces might not be wanted."

Paul was barely restraining himself from grabbing hold of Jake Warner's wife and shaking Marny's whereabouts from her. "Please, I've come a long way, and I'd like to see her –"

"She's feeding the pigs. Come this way, sir." Mrs. Warner crossed the yard and they walked round by the side of the farmhouse, where a few pear trees were shedding fruit into the grass and the odour of pigs was carried strongly on the brisk wind that was blowing. Squealing piglets and snorting, lumbering sows were everywhere, it seemed to Paul, and round by one of the huts a boyish young voice was telling the pigs they'd have her in the troughs in a moment, and she didn't fancy being made a meal of.

Paul's lips twitched; his own inclination slanted very much in that direction.

Mrs. Warner glanced at him. So this, she thought, was the man for whom the lassie was pining. Nice eyes, a bit of a devil's mouth, and from the look of him he'd been doing quite a bit of pining himself.

"Miss Marny's round by the pig houses. I'll leave you to find her, sir."

Mrs. Warner watched Paul walk away, and the November wind blew on her bare arms, still slightly damp from the wash-tub. Jake and his soft heart! She shook her head. He'd lost them a willing pair of hands with that letter of his!

Paul walked round by the pig houses, treading quietly, wanting to see Marny before she saw him. She looked like a boy, with trousers rolled to her knees and an old shapeless jumper falling to her slim hips. Her hair was tied back at the nape of her neck and she stood in a forest of pigs. They were thrusting and bumping into her as she emptied buckets of swill into their troughs, and they did indeed look greedy enough to eat her as well.

"Marny!" Paul said.

He saw her slender body go tense, but she didn't turn round. Her whole attitude was that of someone who didn't dare turn round in case she only dreamed the voice that said her name.

"Marny!" he said again.

The bucket she was holding clattered to the ground and her

young face seemed all green eyes as she swung round. He held open his arms, and wildly, wantingly she fled into them.

It was a dream . . . it was . . . and then she felt the hard arms close bruisingly about her and she was awake for the first time in weeks. Awake. Alive. Her mouth as hungry as the male mouth which had haunted so much of her restless sleep since she had left him to hide herself away from a love she couldn't have.

"Paul! Dearest! Oh, Paul!" She was crying, trembling, certainly not the boy she looked in her trousers and sweater. "I – I'm all piggy. I'll make you smell as awful as I do."

"Chanel Number Five couldn't smell like you at the moment." His eyes and his lips were taking turns at eating her, and Marny couldn't question his sudden, wonderful appearance just yet. She only knew that he still loved and wanted her. He held her so that he made her ache, and she had been wanting to ache like this for weeks.

"You little devil," he whispered shakily, "you ran away and made me the most miserable guy on earth. I've nearly gone out of my mind worrying about you – wondering where you were."

"I – I thought it only fair to leave you." Her tears made wavering lines down her cheeks, for now she felt the pain in him as well as the passion. "How did you find me? And why, Paul – why?"

"I found you because Jake Warner, bless him, thought you needed a man and he wrote to me." Now Paul grinned cheekily at her. "Do you need a man, Miss Lester, honey? Free, white, and though rather past the first flush of boyhood not without a bit of vigour left in him?"

"Paul, tell me what's happened." She had grown suddenly desperate; she was remembering now why she had left him, and it would not be bearable – it would kill her – if she had

186

only dreamed what he had just said to her.

Her face had gone white and he at once grew gentle with her. "It's all right, darling, don't look like that. Ilena set me free. She married Errol Dennis."

Sky and earth whirled together and Marny sank mute against Paul's shoulder. You don't dance for joy when you have heaven, she thought. You want to go down on your knees.

"Sweetheart," Paul touched her, with care, as though she were suddenly made of very precious and breakable porcelain, "aren't you happy?"

"I love you," she whispered. "And now I can love you and I – I'm choked up with it."

The moment was precious, and unbearable, and Paul brought humour to bear. "Do you know, darling, you do smell rather awful," he grinned. But he didn't really seem to mind. His lips found hers and her arms closed hungrily about his neck. After a minute or so, with his lips at her ear lobe, he said: "Will you marry me, you smelly little thing?"

"Mmm, yes!" Her green eyes smiled straight into his. "Fancy dear old Jake writing to you. We met when I first went to London and I told him then that I was going to work for you. What did he say in his letter?"

"He said you were unhappy. He didn't like to see you that way and would I tell your 'young man' where you were." Paul dropped a kiss on her nose, which she wrinkled lovingly. "Your 'young man' is indescribably grateful to dear old Jake Warner. But how come your letters to your aunt always had a London postmark?"

"Jake goes to London once a fortnight to visit his sister, who's a patient at the London Hospital. I wheedled him into posting my letters from there."

"You were really determined to hide yourself away from
187

me, weren't you?"

At once she buried her face against him and he felt her tremble. "I've been so miserable," she whispered. "Sometimes I've had to fight with myself not to come to you, I wanted you so much. If I'd known – oh, if only I'd known it was all over between you and Ilena!"

"Don't fret over it, sweetheart." His lips gently collected the salt of her tears. "We've years ahead of us in which to make up for these past miserable weeks. Now give me a smile and we'll go and tell the Warners that I'm taking you home with me."

"Right this minute, in these awful piggy clothes?"

"Right this minute! I'm not letting you out of my sight ever again. Come along!" His firm arm was around her waist as he marched her away from the grunting, squealing pigs, and his grey eyes smiled happily when he felt her arm go round his waist.

"Did Ginger miss me?" she asked.

"You bet he did. I've had a rare old tussle with Nell Farning and so far I've won the custody of him. I think she'll finally let him go. She knows in her heart that she hasn't anything to give him. We have love to give him, haven't we, my dear?'

Marny smiled up at Paul, while the wind fluttered the tendrils of hair on her forehead and the arm about her tightened possessively.

DISCOVER...

SUPERROMANCE

From the publisher that understands
how you feel about love.

Almost 400 pages of outstanding
romance reading in every book!

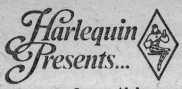

Harlequin Presents...

Choose from this great selection of exciting Harlequin Presents editions

Relive a great romance...
with Harlequin Presents
Complete and mail this coupon today!

Harlequin Reader Service

In the U.S.A.
1440 South Priest Drive
Tempe, AZ 85281

In Canada
649 Ontario Street
Stratford, Ontario N5A 6W2

Please send me the following Harlequin Presents novels. I am enclosing my check or money order for $1.50 for each novel ordered, plus 75¢ to cover postage and handling.

☐ 99	☐ 103	☐ 109
☐ 100	☐ 106	☐ 110
☐ 101	☐ 107	☐ 111
☐ 102	☐ 108	☐ 112

Number of novels checked @ $1.50 each = $_____

N.Y. and Ariz. residents add appropriate sales tax. $_____

Postage and handling $_____ .75

TOTAL $_____

I enclose _____
(Please send check or money order. We cannot be responsible for cash sent through the mail.)

Prices subject to change without notice.

NAME _____
(Please Print)

ADDRESS _____

CITY _____

STATE/PROV. _____

ZIP/POSTAL CODE _____

Offer expires November 30, 1981   105568070